SETTLING DUST

BOOK ONE OF THE MAXWELL CHRONICLES

JACKLYN HENNION

DRAGON EYE
BOOKS

For all the gay witches out there.

CHAPTER

ONE

There was something about downtown Oklahoma City after midnight that I didn't enjoy, and tonight was no exception—far too many people out, many of them half drunk or worse. A bike bar rolled down the street nearby with ten or so people pedaling as they laughed and drank. It seemed like a rolling safety hazard, and I watched as it disappeared from sight. The night was not as dark as it should have been thanks to the countless streetlights and neon signs hanging over eateries and clubs.

But tonight was not the night to judge those who knew how to enjoy themselves. Tonight was my chance to pretend to be just like them. And hopefully get one step closer to what could potentially be the biggest bust of my career.

So I fluffed my hair, adjusted my clothing slightly, and gave the leather bracer on my left forearm and little flick. It buzzed slightly as the arcane energy tied to it responded to the gentle strike.

And then, just for good measure, I double-checked that my badge and gun were still under the glamor spell I'd put on them. They were both tucked into a pocket on the inside of my leather vest, and the spell made the bulk of the weapon impossible to notice.

Once I was sure everything was good to go, I hit the streets of Bricktown.

I heard the music echoing from the club long before I reached the cross street. It was something with a heavy back beat and indistinct lyrics, and I kind of liked it. I found my footsteps naturally falling into rhythm as I reached the crosswalk, and I kept the tempo with light toe taps as I waited for the crossing signal to change. The night was loud and bright, as it always was in Bricktown, and the occasional wind gust brought the smell of fried foods and burgers from the numerous restaurants lining the street.

My stomach rumbled. I should have eaten before coming.

The crossing signal changed, and a stilted robotic voice announced that it was now safe to cross Sheridan Avenue.

I fidgeted with an earring, a large silver stud, and took a deep breath. "Here we go."

Tucking my hands into the pockets of my vest, I jogged the distance to the opposite side.

It was cold, but not so cold that the small heat charms tucked into my pockets didn't instantly erase the sensation when I touched them.

A small line waited at the entrance of Club 405, a group of women significantly more done up and more attractive than me, and I stood by patiently as the bouncer checked IDs and stamped hands. He was a big guy. Big in an *I work out for a living* kind of way. But he also wore glasses, tiny wire frames that only seemed to accent the hugeness of the muscles in his neck and shoulders, and he carried a red felt pen sticking out of a breast pocket with an honest-to-God pocket protector slipped in.

"How's it looking in there?" I asked as I slipped my ID from the sleeve strapped to my arm.

The bouncer shrugged. "It's ladies' night, so it's pretty packed. But the DJ is good, and the light show is set to start again in about ten minutes."

Perfect timing.

He scrutinized my ID for the briefest of moments. Understandable. The woman in the photo was straight-laced and makeup-free. I don't think I was wearing anything brighter than a navy-blue top. And the woman waiting for admittance to the club was wearing fishnets with tall boots and short shorts paired with a hot-pink crop-top halter and pleather vest. I even had a belly-button ring, though he surely couldn't tell it was fake—I had a hard time telling, and I put the damned thing on.

"Ava Maxwell?"

I gave him the cheeriest smile I could muster. "That's me. I, uh, I don't get out much." I shrugged. "And when I do... I go a little crazy."

He passed the ID back and held up a small black stamp. "Just don't get too crazy in there. It'd be a shame to ruin your night so early."

I let him stamp my hand after quickly tucking my ID back into my arm wallet. *Early? It's one in the fucking morning!*

I turned to head into the club, but the bouncer dropped an arm in front of me. "Wait a second."

I froze.

"What's that thing you're wearing?" He pointed to my arm, where my fancy homemade wallet bracer sat snug against the inside of my arm.

"This?" I lifted my arm, thinking quickly. "It's just something I found online. It's got little pockets for cash and cards, and it's so much easier to carry than a purse."

The bouncer shook his head. "I've never seen one before."

I laughed. "Have you ever tried dancing while holding a clutch? I bet these things will be pretty big in a year or two."

Unlikely, but I couldn't admit that I had spent several hours playing with the design and punching far too many holes through the leather. And of course I couldn't mention the shielding spell I'd worked into the piece, either.

"Huh." The bouncer looked from me to the bracer with interest. "It's damn cute. Might have to find one myself."

Something in his voice had changed, and I leaned into it. "Hell, yeah, babe. I love it. And it comes in all kinds of colors."

That got his attention. Another group of women came up behind me, but he ignored them long enough to ask, "Did you see it in pink?"

I laughed again. "I did! Pink would look great on you!"

"Girl, I know." He waved me in. "Don't get too crazy, remember?"

I winked before turning and entering the club.

Well, fuck. I hope someone out there actually makes these.

The inside of the club was much louder, and I took a second to adjust my startled senses to the noise, the smells of alcohol and sweat, and the darkness of the interior. It was packed with people, and my anxiety levels instantly tripled. Like I wasn't already feeling nervous and faintly ill.

What the fuck did I get myself into?

The dance floor was in the center of the room, a huge bar on the adjacent wall closest to the entrance, and a raised stage was at the opposite end. A DJ in a studded BMX helmet was ... doing whatever DJs do. Hitting buttons? Sliding slider things? Making the music happen, whatever it was. And though I had no idea what he was up to, it sounded great. Or so I thought. And the dance floor was full of swaying bodies, so I must not have been the only one who thought so.

I shuffled through the dozen or so tables that separated me from the bar and stopped at the counter. A bartender arranged half a dozen shots onto a metal tray held by a slim-waisted girl in shorts shorter than mine and sent her off with a nod towards a table full of ladies.

"Whatchu need?" he asked, arranging another half dozen shot glasses in a row with a speed I was honestly envious of.

"Is Jack back there?" I asked with a smile and a finger pointed at the well in front of him.

He snorted as if he hadn't heard that same joke a million times already. "Jack is always back here." He lifted a familiar bottle and held it up for me to see. "Single, double?"

"Single."

"Four dollars."

For a shot of Jack Daniels? Shit.

I dropped a five on the counter. "Keep the change."

He slapped the bill and made it disappear, then slid a shot glass with a finger's width of liquid my way.

I could have drunk the shot, but the last thing I needed was to get an earful for drinking on the job. I needed the lingering stink of alcohol on me, and there was an easy way to get that without doing any actual imbibing. No one at the bar was staring directly at me. The bartender already had his attention elsewhere, and most of the people waiting to place orders were women standing in small clusters and chatting amicably and in close quarters.

So I dipped the tips of two fingers into the drink and dabbed a little Jack behind both ears. Then I did the same to my collarbones for good measure.

And then I set to surveilling the club.

The end of the bar was next to a staircase of dark wood and carpeted stairs, and I glanced up to the balcony to see a couple of women dancing in a lazy, drunken way. One held a martini glass, and I wondered how they managed to prevent drops and spills from raining down on guests on the ground floor. No sooner had the thought finished processing when the woman holding the martini glass made to set her drink down on the balcony rail and missed terribly. The drink fell a good ten feet before hitting a thick sheet of clear plexiglass covering the tables and bar area below with a series of bounces and plastic clinks.

The bartender glanced up at the plastic martini glass, which on closer inspection was a bright pink, and continued pouring drinks without a pause. A champagne flute, likely also plastic, lay not far from where the martini glass had settled.

The martini drinker wailed something unintelligible and stared down at her lost drink with a pout.

Clubs, man. They bring out an interesting class of characters.

When I left the bar, I left what was evidently about three-and-a-half dollars' worth of well liquor behind.

I made for the stairs to the balcony, but stopped when a second bouncer positioned there held out a hand. "Private party, no one allowed."

This guy was smaller than the bouncer outside, but not by much. And what he lacked in the slight nerd department he more than made up for by being incredibly intimidating.

"I'm looking for my boyfriend." I rubbernecked the balcony, giving it a cursory sweep. "Do you mind if I look for him up there really quick?"

He didn't budge. "No men up here. Private party."

Okayyy ...

I thought of flashing my badge, but I wasn't entirely convinced the Neanderthal before me would be able to comprehend that an officer of the law was requesting access. Plus, I didn't want word to spread that a cop was on the scene.

So I stamped a foot and made a face, then turned on my heels and walked off for the bathrooms.

The bathrooms were easy to find, and I fiddled with my earring again on the way to the ladies' room. There were no doors, just a little doorway for each side with a beer pint over one and a wine glass over the other.

I eyed the wineglass sign over the women's room. "Sexist."

By some miracle, the room was empty.

"Did you get that sweep?" I said softly.

A voice crackled in my ear. "I got it. Checking now."

I primped my hair a bit, admiring the wild tangle of black curls it had been styled into.

"Balcony is clear. And you look lovely, Maxwell."

"Don't think I won't kick your ass in these boots, Jackson."

A gaggle of women stepped in and instantly made for the sinks.

Wow, it really is ladies' night.

I gave the stud earring a twist again and shut off the arcane comm line running from it to the officer waiting two blocks away. On my way back to the club, I debated having a quick peek inside the men's room. I ultimately decided against it. My mark was likely on the dance floor, and I didn't want to fake drunkenness any more than absolutely necessary tonight. Though the stupid men's and women's signs might be enough to excuse away stepping into the wrong bathroom.

"Oh, excuse me, I didn't realize I'm supposed to stick to

gendered norms regarding alcoholic beverages in this day and age."

Not that I don't like wine. I just happen to also like beer.

A third door was located at the end of the hall, but there was a keypad on it and a sign that read 'Employees Only', so I didn't even bother checking the knob.

The light show was just getting started when I reached the bar again. The lights over the dance floor were doused, and a series of black lights and neon lasers shot over the crowd, pulsing to the beat of the DJ's latest track. There were no empty tables, so I took to carefully wandering the edge of the dance floor, searching the crowd. It didn't take long to find the guy I wanted. The spiked hair helped quite a lot—it picked up the black light and flashed from what looked in the darkness to be a dark red to a bright orange.

He was currently trying his moves on a dark-skinned woman who looked a little young to be where she was, but she wasn't having it. I slipped between them before she could let off an almighty slap and gave her the *get away, girl, I got you* look that comes naturally to all women.

Dude didn't even notice when she left. He just kept grinding away, only now it was on me.

Gross.

We kept at it. He had been drinking, I could smell it on his breath. And maybe he could smell the whiskey I'd dabbed on my neck. He got handsy superfast. I matched him, slipping my hands under his shirt and up his abdomen. He was really sweaty.

So gross.

And then I groped his ass. To be fair, he grabbed mine first. And I was actually feeling his back pockets. They were both empty. Which meant the goods were in his front pockets, and I wasn't about to start feeling around there.

To make it worse, he had a nice butt.

I turned my grimace into a smile.

He gave me a doped-up smile in return.

"My name is Ava," I shouted.

"Hi, Ava!" he shouted back.

The music was winding down, or so it seemed. It was hard for me to be sure, but the lights were less frequent and their pulses were growing softer.

"You want to take this party somewhere else?" I asked, slipping a couple of fingers of each hand into the waistband of his jeans. It wasn't difficult. His jeans were pretty loose and baggy. And was he wearing tighty-whities?

Dude, come on.

"Hell, yeah! There's a VIP balcony in the back I can get us into."

"It's already booked." I gave him a deep, pouting frown.

"Well, damn." He scanned the bar area over my head. "Tables are full, too." He arched an eyebrow. "Bathroom will be empty."

Classy.

I shrugged. "Maybe it's not worth it."

"Oh, no, don't say that. I've got some good shit that will really make it a party."

"Yeah? What's that?"

He reached into a front pocket—his left one, I noted— and pulled out a tiny vial of lilac-colored powder.

"Is that Dust?" I asked, my mouth open in wonder.

"Sure is, baby. You ever try it?"

I shook my head. "Where did you even get some? I've never seen it."

He smiled, his eyes slightly unfocused. "I know the guy that handles the supply."

Gotcha, bitch.

I gave him a wink. "The bathroom it is, then."

Letting him lead the way, I kept a close eye on him as he

moved. Dude was either stupid or high or both. He didn't even ask if I was a cop, though I guess he did get his hands on me long enough to tell I wasn't wired. Not in the conventional way, anyway. He'd kept his hands far enough from the pocket of my jacket to not feel my gun, but the glamor would have messed with his perception of it anyway. If the drugs he was on didn't do so first.

The men's bathroom was just as clean as the women's, surprisingly. I fully expected shit-stained walls and piss puddles on the floor. But it was pristine and even smelled faintly of something floral. It must not have been used much yet today. Or maybe the club really did keep it that nice as much as possible.

And it was totally empty.

Thankfully, the door did not lock, but there were three stalls at the far end of the room, beyond a row of bleach-white urinals.

We very swiftly ended up in the center stall, with the door latched shut behind us. It was roomy, and Mr. Handsy quickly dispensed with his pants, leaving his shoes on.

"So, you deal Dust for a living?"

"Sure do, babe. What about you?" He tugged his shirt over his head, barely breaking his over-gelled hair spikes, which were actually a deep sunset orange.

"I work for OKAPD." I pulled a pair of handcuffs out of the inner pocket of my vest.

"What's that?" He spotted the cuffs and his eyes glinted. "You into that kind of shit, babe?"

"I work for the Oklahoma Arcane Police Department, you idiot. I'm arresting you."

Mr. Handsy finally seemed to get everything clicked together as I snapped one ring of the cuffs around his left wrist.

"Fuck."

He went in with a headbutt, which landed on my shoulder. Blood instantly gushed from his nose.

"Wow, you really are an idiot."

The possibly broken nose did not deter him, and he swung with his dominant hand, which happened to be the left, as I noted when he reached for the vial of Pixie Dust in his pants, and which was now cuffed.

I caught the swing easily and turned it into a slam against the side of the stall. "Roger Feldman, you're under arrest for being a terrible dancer, for being far too comfortable with touching women you do not know, and for overusing hair gel. And also for possession with intent to distribute. And probably a whole bunch of other shit that I'll get sorted out soon enough." I fought to get the cuff around his other wrist, but Feldman was being too wriggly and sweaty.

"Fuck you, bitch!"

"Like I haven't heard that one before."

He came back with a head slam, and this time it landed in a place far more inconvenient for me. I fell back against the opposite wall of the stall, momentarily dazed by the hair spike that almost took my eye out. Feldman turned, reaching for me. He was several inches taller than me, and the only good visual I got was of two huge hands, one dangling a silver set of handcuffs, coming right for me.

I sprayed him in the face with a perfume bottle I'd tucked into another inner pocket of my vest.

He stumbled back, surprised, and I quickly covered my mouth and slipped through the stall door.

Feldman didn't follow.

Instead, he started violently vomiting into the toilet.

I waited a few seconds for the potion I'd misted into the bathroom to dissipate before uncovering my mouth.

The stall door had swung shut behind me, and when I

cautiously opened it, Feldman was on his knees, mostly naked, hugging the porcelain toilet and loudly heaving bile.

I calmly reached over him and latched the remaining cuff to his right hand, looping it through the exposed plumping.

"What'd you do to me?" he managed between heaves.

"Vomiting potion. It'll wear off in just a minute."

Feldman spat bile and blood into the toilet and wiped his face on the inside of an arm. "Bitch."

"I know." I fished his pants from the floor and reached into the left front pocket, hoping the vial of Dust was still intact after the scuffle. It was, and I held it up to inspect.

I quickly adjusted the stud in my ear again. "You getting this, Benji?"

"Fuck, Maxwell. Why'd you wreck the guy so hard?" Officer Benjamin Jackson's voice came over the comm line with a slight crackle. "I don't want to deal with some dude vomiting in the back of my cruiser."

"He'll stop vomiting in a minute, man. Just come and get him. I'm heading back to town to get this looked at."

"What? You can't leave, Ava. We've got protocol to follow."

"I know protocol. And I'm saying I'm floating it. I need to make sure this is the real shit." I sighed, pocketing the vial and reaching for the comm again. "Just cover for me, Benji. I need four hours. Six, tops."

I shut the comm off before he could respond and left the bathroom.

The hallway leading back to the dance floor was empty, and I realized that the door behind me had done a remarkable job of dampening the sound of the music in the club.

I got all the way down to the end of the hall and turned the corner before bumping into anyone else. And then I quite literally bumped into someone else. The hall was too dark to make out a face, but I gave a quick apology before slipping around him and heading for the door.

Mercifully, the bouncer was gone. I didn't have it in me to make up another lie on the spot about my wallet, and I could feel a bruise forming around my eye socket where Feldman's head had met my face.

Traffic was light enough at Sheridan that I didn't even wait for the cross light to come on. The robotic voice was silent as I hurried to the opposite side, hands now wrapped around the heat charms and the small vial of Pixie Dust. A huge parking garage was conveniently right across from Club 405, and I had been lucky enough to find a spot on the third floor for my motorcycle.

I was gunning it down the parking ramp and headed back to the highway within five minutes.

CHAPTER

TWO

The drive from Oklahoma City to Norman, Oklahoma, is an easy one. At two in the morning, that is. During rush hours it's just as miserable and frustrating as any other highway or interstate can be. But in the early morning hours, when the moon is high in the sky and there's hardly any traffic, the ride is almost relaxing.

Tonight it gave me plenty of time to internally freak the hell out over the little vial of powder I had in my pocket.

Fucking Pixie Dust. Such an innocuous and even cute name for something that was causing panic and mayhem all over the metro.

The street drug had first appeared not quite a year ago as little more than a whisper. Now there were numerous deaths and countless unexplained phenomena associated with the drug. And the ten grams or so I had confiscated from Roger Feldman was more than enough to add to those numbers if it had been distributed to the streets.

Not only had I confiscated it, but I'd made the biggest arrest on the case to date. And all it took was a borrowed outfit and a good deal of my dignity. The outfit would be returned soon. And my dignity would heal as soon as I could shower and get the smell of Feldman and club atmosphere off my skin.

My ride ended a little more than twenty miles south from where it began, at the University of Oklahoma's campus. More specifically, I parked my motorcycle—a Blackbird inherited from my father—in the southeast corner of their event center and made the brisk walk over to the life sciences building across the street. The research center was pretty impressive and still had that new-building look. Even the inside was still nearly perfect, though it usually smelled faintly of weird science experiments and stale coffee.

The doors should have all been locked—it was only just after two thirty in the morning—but I knew a side door that was usually left unlocked. Mostly for me, if I'm being honest. Two thirty a.m. trips to a certain chemistry PhD's office were not unheard of for me. It was, frankly, the best time to find the guy.

His office was empty apart from papers scattered about on just about every surface but the path from the door to a faded green couch and the couch itself. I dropped my helmet on a stack of typed lab reports, the top one of which was covered in red ink and had a large 47 penned and circled next to the title. There was a half eaten cup of noodles and a mug of black coffee, and I helped myself to some of each. Both were cold but gave off the impression of being recently warm, so they didn't make me gag outright.

What is it that they say about people that drink black coffee? That they're either brilliant people without the time to even prepare and enjoy a proper cup of coffee, or they're psychopaths. I was pretty sure Frankie was in that first group, but there was still a small chance he was in the second.

I doffed my jacket vest, draped it over my helmet, and polished off the coffee. The green couch called to me, and I gave it a longing look before leaving the office behind.

"Soon, my sweet."

Yeah, I'd spent my share of early morning hours passed out on that poor thing. It was lumpy and sat directly beneath a vent, but damn did it put you to sleep quick.

Frankie was precisely where I thought he would be. I could see his ruffled hair poking out from behind a computer monitor and hear indistinct muttering of what were likely Spanish insults.

"Frankie, I've got another one for you," I called as I crossed the room. The heavy smell of some sort of alcohol hung in the air. Not the fun kind, like the whiskey that was probably still wafting around my collarbones. The medical and science kind. The "don't drink or you'll go blind" kind.

"Hey, Ava!" Frankie stood up, but he didn't look away from the computer right away. "You get your guy?"

"I got one of the guys. The big one is still out there."

"You'll find him, girl." He finally looked up and his eyes instantly widened. "Damn, hussy. I'm surprised you only got one guy tonight."

"Who said I stopped at one?" I put a hand on a hip and tossed my wind-stricken hair.

"The fact that it's almost three in the morning and you're here instead of rolling around in some stranger's bed."

I frowned. "Ass."

He came around the desk, scrutinizing my outfit. "That top looks damn good though. I mean, it looks better on Dorian, but you make it work."

"This is Dorian's top? I thought it was yours." I quickly checked for any damage to the pink halter.

"Please, I wouldn't be caught dead wearing that. It

looks so tacky." Frankie returned to the monitor, frowning at the screen.

"Don't loan me your boyfriend's clothes, Frankie. What if I got something spilled on it?"

"Dorian wore that to a bubble rave in Austin two months ago. If it can survive that, it can survive whatever sad evening you had."

I frowned, unsure if I should be insulted or relieved. I didn't even know what a bubble rave was. But Frankie and Dorian were much more attuned to the various club scenes than I ever planned to be. If Frankie thought it was fine, it must be fine.

I sighed, coming to stand behind Frankie's shoulder. "Tell him thank you, and that I owe him one. I'll return the top and the hair styler he loaned me this weekend."

"Mhm." Frankie was staring at a strange graph on his screen. It looked like a bunch of weird lines to me, but Frankie seemed to know what he was looking at. He shook his head, muttering under his breath.

"Problem?"

"Yeah, I've got a student with shit for brains." The slight Hispanic accent to his words made the phrase sound more amusing than anything else.

"Ready for a break?"

Frankie pushed his chair back and sighed. "Yeah. I think I left a cup of coffee in my office. I should finish it before it gets cold."

"Oof, too late, bro."

Frankie groaned. "Did you eat my ramen, too?"

"Not all of it." I gave him my most innocent smile.

"Alright, then show me what you got while I finish those. Can't let you get your greedy little claws on them again."

Back in Frankie's office, I sat on the green couch and

fished the Dust from my jacket while Frankie inspected his noodles and empty coffee cup with a pout.

Frankie ate his noodles alarmingly fast. I passed the vial of Dust over to him while he slurped the last noods up. "If you can run a couple of tests on this for me, I'd owe you big time. Just enough to determine that it's the same stuff I brought you last time."

Frankie held the vial up to inspect. "This the Pixie Glitter shit you been talking about?"

"Pixie Dust," I corrected.

"Right, right. Just a pinch to make you fly, yeah?"

"That's what they've been saying."

Frankie squinted at the Dust. "Is this really all that bad? It looks like something you would use to decorate macaroni art."

"It's killed eight people in the last three months, Frankie. Just here in town. And we can't figure out how."

Frankie nodded. "Right. The drug and arcane blend."

"Those deaths aren't conventional drug overdoses." I pointed at the vial in Frankie's hand. "Something in that is wreaking havoc in the community in ways the mundane drug task force just can't comprehend. And I need your help figuring out what it is."

"Alright, alright. Don't get preachy on me." He rubbed his face and palmed the vial. "I'll do a GC-MS and an NMR to help identify the chemical structure. At the very least, we can quickly determine if it matches the last vial of confetti you brought me."

"I don't know what any of that means, but thanks, Frankie." I settled down on the couch, propping my feet up one end and resting my head against the other.

"And then you're taking the rest down to the district's lab for the *professionals* to handle, right?"

I snorted. "Yeah, so they can get results back to me in

six months." I closed my eyes, draping my arm over my head to block out the fluorescent light streaming in from the hallway. "Those assholes keep giving me the runaround. They still haven't tested the last vial I sent in."

"You want a blankie, Princess?" Frankie asked in a mocking tone.

"Yeah, if you've got one."

"Check the floor." His voice was fading. He'd already left for the lab.

I took a quick peek from under my arm at the floor. Beneath the coffee table that was currently serving as a sad memoriam to undergraduate hopes of passing chemistry lab was a quilted blanket wadded into a ball and piled high with notebooks and a small collection of cheap red pens. I thought about carefully dislodging it, but the AC unit had kicked on somewhere in the building and a soft chill came from the vent above me. Instead I just yanked the quilt from beneath the table and quickly burrito'd myself inside.

* * *

It was incredibly cold. Cold enough that I couldn't feel my feet, but I was too scared to be concerned about that. Water flooded in through the cracks in the windshield and through the twisted frame of the car. It was muddy and heavy with silt and stank of rotting fish. And it was deeply cold.

"Ava." A man's hand gripped my upper arm, pulling me briefly away from the rear window, where I had been pounding ineffectively against the glass. "Ava, help me get your brother out of his car seat."

My father had blood on the side of his face. His hair was plastered to his head, as were his clothes. He'd been wearing a white button-up, and it was dirty from the blood and the filthy lake water.

I clambered over the center seat to the one my little brother's car seat was fastened into. He wasn't crying, and his head and arms lolled forward towards the front of the car, which was now stuck to the earthy bottom of Lake Thunderbird. His little legs were already submerged.

"Hold his head up." My father fumbled with the belts of the seat, his hands disappearing into the murk. "Keep him out of the water."

I did as I was told, holding Alex's head up with one hand and the weight of his limp body with the other. I usually hated having to carry him, but I did so now without complaint.

There was a lot of tugging; I could feel it in the way the car seat jerked against me, and then Alex was free. I held him close, letting his head fall against my shoulder like he was sleeping.

My father climbed over the third row of seats in our family's minivan and helped me over. Water had almost covered Alex's car seat, and I heard the car groaning. I leaned back against the back of the seat, staring out of the rear windshield. All I could see was brown. There was no light, only the disturbed silt from the impact.

"Ava, listen."

I turned to my father. He was also leaning against the rear row of seats, but his feet were positioned against the back window. "I'm going to kick the window out. It'll break, but not at first. When it's about to go, I'm going to count to three. On three, you take a deep breath and swim out of the car and up to the surface, okay?"

He wasn't looking at me. He was looking through the window, maybe wondering the same things I was. How deep were we? Which way was up?

"What about Alex?"

He turned to face me. His face was drawn and pale, like he'd just realized there was no way he could save both of us. No way to get us both out of there.

"You hold on to Alex, and I'll pull you up with me. Just promise you'll hold on to him for me. Don't let go of him."

I nodded. "Please don't leave me, Daddy."

He started kicking. It took two kicks, aimed at the center of the glass, to get cracks started. Water immediately began seeping in, and I watched the cracks quickly spread.

"One," my father said.

I shifted my grip on Alex. I felt water tickling my back.

"Two."

The window broke and water rushed in. I had enough time to take a deep breath before it hit me and pressed me against the seats.

I struggled against the current of the incoming water, reaching blindly for the rear frame of the van. I couldn't see anything in the water, and I felt grit in my eyes. I stumbled through the broken window, and immediately began kicking my feet blindly and pawing upward with one hand. I had been swimming, but never in the deep end of the pool. And this was nothing like a pool.

And then I felt that same strong hand grab me around the upper arm again, this time pulling me through the water. I was pulled in a different direction than I had been trying to go, and an echoing crunch from very close to my head told me I had not left the van very far behind. It was now resting fully on the bottom of the lake, and more sand and dirt bloomed up around me.

I kept kicking my legs, holding Alex close to my chest and trying not to fight the grip on my arm even though my shoulder burned.

My lungs began to ache, and I closed my eyes to ignore the shadow of black that was creeping into my vision.

It was so cold.

"Ava, wake up. I've got some results ready."

I jerked away at Frankie's touch on my arm. "Shit, Frankie. Don't scare me like that."

"Maybe if you hadn't buried yourself in the covers, you may have heard me say your name the first time and I wouldn't have to touch your clammy-ass arm." He pushed at my legs, and I gave him room to sit down. He held a fresh cup of coffee in his hand.

I sat up. "Is that for me?"

He gave me a look. "No." And then he handed me the cup.

It was black, and I took a huge gulp before passing it back to him. "What time is it?"

"Five thirty. The place is going to start filling up soon. You'll have to head out before someone realizes I'm housing a prostitute in my office."

"What have you got for me?" I nodded at the slip of paper he held.

"An XRD scan." He passed it over to me. "And a tissue. Your eyeliner is running." He tugged a small tissue from a green and white box. Not strictly the kind of tissue you would normally wipe tears away with, but it worked fine. I wiped under each eye while Frankie sat and patiently drank his coffee.

I didn't have the heart to tell Frankie that I'd dreamt of my brother's and father's deaths during those two short hours of sleep, but I'm sure he realized what was up. He knew about the occasional nightmares, and had seen me in the midst of them more than once. But Frankie was not the type to hold me while I cried. He said he left that kind of gay shit up to Dorian.

I looked the report over. Several color-coded lines matched up with a variety of spikes on a graph. The legend listed some drug names that I had become familiar with. "Alright, I see at least two narcotics, a few uppers, and … glucose?"

Frankie nodded. "Sugar. To make it sweet."

"Right. Dust is supposed to be ingested, not inhaled or injected." I pointed at a couple of indistinct areas of the graph. The peaks here were short and broad, unlike everything else. "What's this? There's no ID for these two spots."

Frankie pointed at the first one, on the far left of the graph. "That one indicates something amorphous in the drug. Something that doesn't have a crystalline structure. Not completely unexpected, even if the stuff does look like glitter. And the area under the curve is small, so my guess would be a fairly small amount of whatever."

"And the other one?" I pointed at the second area, which was much larger than the first and took up much of the last quarter of the graph.

Frankie shrugged. "I don't know. I've never seen anything like that. Something that's fluorescing, maybe? Or something else that's screwing up the scan?" He took a sip of his coffee. "It was in the last scan, too."

"So this is the same stuff?"

"Whatever it is, I hope your guys at the district lab have better luck than I did." He returned the vial of Dust with a skeptical look at the contents.

"Is this the only test you did?"

"It's the only one that's finished. I need more time for the rest. I have to put the students' samples above yours, I'm afraid. But it'll get done by lunch."

"Thanks, Frankie. Come by my house later and you can explain everything to me then."

"Buy me tacos, and I'll think about coming over."

I stood up and stretched. "You've got a deal."

My fake belly-button ring chose that moment to fall out, which elicited a snort from both of us. Frankie picked it up and held it out for me. "I think you dropped this."

I pocketed the jewelry and grabbed my jacket. "I'll be so happy to get home and change."

I exited the life sciences building the same way I came in. The sun was still a ways off from rising, but the parking lot across the street was already looking fuller. It was still chilly, and the sweat on my arm and the back of my neck faded.

I got a strong side-eye from an older woman in a pair of slacks and a blouse as I hurried across the parking lot of the life sciences building and to the street. I also got a few laughs from a young pair of college students.

I gave the students a nod. "Thirsty Thursday ran a little late."

That only made them laugh more.

Like I could still pass for a college student.

I chose jaywalking over waiting on the side of the street and risking more laughter and stares. Maybe my dignity would take a little longer to recover than I thought.

I heard a familiar electronic jingle as I neared my Blackbird, and I cursed. I quickly fished my cell phone out of the tail bag and answered it without looking too closely at the caller ID. "Maxwell here."

"Where the fuck have you been, Maxwell?"

It was the district captain, Ellis Ross. And he sounded pissed.

"I was following up on a lead from last night's arrest, sir." It was far from the truth, but also not entirely a lie.

"And what lead would that be, Maxwell?"

I hesitated.

"We do not use civilians to run tests on dangerous materials or assist in dangerous investigations."

He knew I'd been with Frankie. I could only sigh.

"Tell Mr. Alvarez to immediately stop any tests he is performing and to discard his results. The samples will be brought to me as soon as possible."

"Of course, sir." I had no intention of doing anything of the sort.

"In the meantime, you need to get your ass down here and do some explaining."

"Explain what?" My voice came out a little testy, and I'm sure he noticed.

"Explain how your arrest last night led to the death of the suspect."

My breath caught. "W-what?"

"Feldman is dead, Maxwell. And you were the last one to see him alive."

CHAPTER

THREE

I hightailed it for headquarters, cursing all the while. How had Feldman died? He was fine when I left him. Aside from the vomiting, obviously. And that wouldn't have killed him. He was clearly on some sort of drug—it could have been an overdose.

Or a bad reaction to the drug mixed with the vomiting potion ...

Shit.

Or he may have just been really drunk, and not on drugs at all. Not all dealers used.

Those thoughts and more swam through my head as I wove my way through the Norman streets. It was still early enough that traffic was light, and it took little time for me to cross town again.

Norman's police department was located in the center of town. Their mundane, non-magical department, anyway. I didn't technically work for NPD.

OKAPD, on the other hand, was a quasi-secluded and secretive department. Rather than policing individual cities, OKAPD policed the entire state. We had offices in the

26

largest cities—Oklahoma City and Tulsa to the northeast. There were a few smaller offices scattered throughout the more remote areas to the west, plus a nice office that staffed two officers and a detective up in the panhandle that I'd visited once. They were stretched pretty thin and trying to cover all three panhandle counties plus the western half of Harper County. Doing that simple math, it came out to less than one officer per county. And being the remotest part of Oklahoma, it tended to get pretty freaky out there when it came to arcane work. The two officers were a husband and wife duo with awesome evocation talent of which I was in awe. The detective, a Cherokee by the name of Inola, was a hilarious and kind herbal arcanist. Those guys were a brilliant close-knit team. I was happy to work with them, and I would gladly do so again if the chance ever arose.

My office was the one located in OKC. We were the largest office, both in size and in staff, and we policed the largest district in terms of square mileage. It covered all the OKC metro, down as far south as Noble and north up to Edmond. That came to almost 6,400 square miles, and nearly one and a half million people. Even just thinking of the sheer number of people in the metro area with some degree of arcane ability made my eyes water.

My job was to make sure they used those abilities legally and without alerting the mundane communities that there were those out in the world who looked and acted just like them, but who were able to do things they could only ever dream of. Rules and laws existed governing what an arcanist could and couldn't do publicly, or even privately, and most of those laws were to help keep our existence as low-key as possible.

It had its good days. And it had its bad days. And today was looking like it was going to be a bad day.

The OKAPD office looked like any run-of-the-mill boring government building. Brown brick, nondescript exterior, and a single sign with our acronym on it and the state seal. No further explanation of what we did or who we were. Exactly as expected from a state agency. No one knew why half of them existed, and they didn't really care as long as their taxes didn't go up.

The parking lot was almost empty. I spotted Benjamin's old beat-up Camry in a back corner, and his black APD cruiser was parked in front of the building under a metal awning, right next to Captain Ross's personal vehicle, an oversized white Lexus that looked like it was washed and waxed every single day.

I groaned inside my helmet.

I parked my bike in one of the spots closest to the front door and ran in as fast as my heeled boots would let me. I felt absolutely ridiculous in my outfit, and the officer on guard duty didn't bother to hide his smile at all as he checked my badge and waved me through the scanner.

"Nice uniform, Maxwell."

"Go to hell, Pendle."

Captain Ross's office was in the back of the building, and I had to walk through four different hallways and the central office space to get to it. Only one officer noticed me, thankfully, and it was the one officer I wanted to find before meeting with Ross anyway.

Benjamin stood up from his desk at the sight of me. "Ava, where the hell you been? I tried calling and texting. You never answered."

"I left my cell on my bike." I stopped in front of him, trying to use his body to block the open window to Ross's office so I wouldn't be spotted right away. But Ross was waiting, and he immediately stood up and went for the door. "What the hell happened, Benji?"

"I was hoping you could tell me. I went to the bathroom to bring him in, and the dude was dead."

Ross stepped outside the door to his office. "Maxwell. Now."

"How? Overdose?" I quickly asked Benji, stepping around him.

Benji shook his head. "Definitely not."

"Jackson, back to work. You're in enough trouble as it is," Ross bellowed.

"Yes, sir," Benji answered, and I turned to catch him slipping back into his chair, dejected.

Ross held the door open for me and waved me in. "What the hell are you wearing, detective?"

"I'm sorry, sir. I haven't had the chance to go home and change. This is what I wore to get the arrest last night." I was surprised to see another person in the office, someone I didn't recognize. He wore a sensible suit and tie, and his dark hair was trimmed close and styled neatly. I stopped short, immediately feeling even more ridiculous and highly embarrassed.

Ross sighed heavily. "Take a seat, Maxwell. This is Detective Howell."

Howell extended a hand, and we shook.

"What office are you from, Howell?" I tried tugging my shirt down to cover a little more of my ass as I sat in the chair beside him. If Howell noticed, he made no sign.

Howell opened his mouth to answer, but Ross cut him off. "Detective Howell is SIU. He's tasked with the FBI and is here for the Pixie Dust investigation."

Special Investigations, huh? And with FBI credentials.

"So, we're getting federal help?" I asked, surprised.

"Not exactly, Detective," Howell said. He had a surprisingly deep voice that didn't quite suit his frame. "I'm taking the investigation over."

"What?" I stood, glaring from Howell to Ross. "You can't take the investigation from me. I've been on this thing for eight months!"

"And in that eight months, you have made three arrests, one minor drug conviction, and your latest suspect died under mysterious circumstances after you left him cuffed at the scene." Ross's face grew very red, a sure sign something very bad was about to happen.

But I pressed further. "Feldman was going to lead me to the manufacturer, I'm sure of it."

"And Feldman is dead, Detective." He stabbed a finger in my direction. "So far, all the evidence we have points to you."

I fell into my chair again. Howell had remained silent, staring at nothing.

"Are you saying Feldman was murdered?"

"I'm saying," Ross continued, his voice only marginally calmer, "that the investigation is still ongoing. And as the last one to see him alive—"

"I'm the prime suspect."

"Tell us what happened, Detective Maxwell," Howell said. "Help us understand."

So I told them. All the way up to returning to the parking garage across from Club 405. I left out no details.

"And you met no one on the way out of the club?"

"No." Then I remembered the man in the hallway outside the bathrooms. "Actually, yeah. I bumped into someone. On the way back to the dance floor."

Howell made a note in the pad he held. "And the bouncer? Did he see you on the way out?"

"Nah." I sighed, rubbing at my face. "He wasn't there when I left."

Howell frowned and made another note.

"And then you went down to campus and asked your friend Alvarez to test the Dust you got from Feldman," Ross said.

"It was just to see if it was the same stuff we picked up last time."

"Still, you took evidence to a civilian and asked them to test it." Ross's face was getting red again.

"It was just one test," I protested. A bold lie, but one I had no intention of disproving.

"And what did this Mr. Alvarez determine?" Howell asked.

I let out a calming sigh, ignoring the glare Ross was giving me to focus instead on Howell. "That they were the same. And that he's not able to determine what the drug is, exactly."

Howell closed his pad. "You understand that I'm going to need that report, right?"

I nodded. "I'll get it to you as soon as I can."

Howell stood. "I think that's all I need from your detective, Ellis. I'll be at the crime scene for the next few hours if you need me."

"I'll make sure you get everything we have on this, Phil."

First-name basis. I am fucked.

Howell left without a backwards glance. I watched him until he was about halfway across the central office, when Ross brought my attention back to him.

"Now, about your reprimand."

Fuck.

"Sir, I'm sorry about what happened. I have no excuse or explanation."

"I know you don't." Ross stood again, crossing his arms over his chest. The dude worked out a lot, so it was kind of intimidating to see. "You admitted to several different infractions during your verbal report to Howell." He grimaced. "Most importantly, leaving a suspect cuffed to a toilet and pulling out before backup arrived." The grimace turned into a disapproving scowl. "And then this business with Alvarez handling the Dust. Any defense attorney could argue contamination or mishandling of evidence or a dozen other things."

"I just wanted answers, Ross. And you know it takes our guys forever. The trail would be cold by the time we figured out what Dust actually is."

"Doesn't matter." Ross shook his head. He held out a hand. "You're on suspension until this investigation is over."

Fuck.

"Which investigation? Feldman's death, or the Dust investigation?"

Ross shrugged. "I don't know. Whichever takes longer."

Fuck, fuck, fuck.

"Fine." I stood, pulling my badge from my jacket and dropping it onto his desk. My gun I carefully pulled from the shoulder holster I'd returned it to after leaving Club 405, checked the safety was still off, and passed it over to Ross.

"Go home, Maxwell. Get some rest. And change your clothes, for crying out loud."

"Can I at least review the autopsy notes on Feldman's death?"

Ross scoffed. "Hell no. You'll be kept apprised of the investigation as I see fit."

Which meant not at all.

We'll see about that.

"Fine," I repeated with a sigh. "I just need to grab a few things from my desk and I'll be gone."

Ross watched me as I left his office. I felt his angry little eyes boring into the back of my skull. Also, the dude was a talented arcane user, from what I'd heard. And that kind of energy gives off ... well, energy. You could feel it when someone with that kind of juju juice was focusing their attention on you. Like, actually feel it. It was unsettling in a lot of cases. Maybe romantic under the right ones.

This was not the romantic kind.

This was the "I'm watching you, Maxwell, so don't fuck up or I'm canning your sorry ass" kind.

I've gotten somewhat accustomed to it over my time with OKAPD.

The sensation disappeared instantly when I shut the door to his office. I stopped by Officer Jackson's desk and took a quick peek over my shoulder to see Ross shuffling through a report on his desk.

"What'd you get?" Benji asked in a low voice.

"Suspension."

"Damn."

"Yeah. I can't even look at the case files."

Benji snorted. "I mean, that's what a suspension is."

I leaned against the edge of his desk, keeping my focus split between Ross and my friend. My buddy, my pal, my saving grace.

"I need you to look at any new files that come in on this Dust case and fill me in."

Benji groaned. "No, Ava."

"Please?"

"No." His voice was not firm. Not a bit.

"Pretty please?"

He shook his head. He couldn't even bring himself to voice an outright refusal.

It was so easy to wear him down that I honestly felt guilty about it.

"I'll take you to that golfing place you like for your birthday. You can drink all the overpriced beers you want."

"My birthday is in three months, Ava. Try harder."

Ooh, hardball.

I smiled. "I'll take you as soon as my suspension is over. And you can throw in an overpriced meal as well as the beer."

Benji's eyes narrowed. "Three hours of drive time."

Ugh, he really knows how to bargain.

"Deal."

We shook on it. I stood, giving him a soft pat on the back. "Start with the autopsy report on Feldman. I want to know what killed him."

Benji snorted. "That one's easy. His neck was broken." He shook his head, an ill look coming over his face. "It was bad."

I chewed my lip. *Shit.*

"Tell me anything else you can as soon as you can. My ass is on this one, Benji." I tapped the earring I still wore; the comm line was still closed but could be opened with a simple twist of the stone set into the stud. "I'll be keeping an ear out for you, bud."

"What if Ross listens in?"

"I'm on suspension." I rolled my eyes. "Why would he listen in on my comm line?"

I went home.

It was one of those drives where you zone out just a little bit and actually drive the speed limit, ignoring everyone and everything around you, head down and nose to the ground, fatigued by the world. My anger about the suspension and Feldman's death and losing my Pixie Dust bust to some Special Investigations guy with fed papers and a nice suit had subsided into a melancholic resignation. Plus, I was exhausted. I spent the drive home thinking of exactly three things: a hot shower, some comfortable clothes, and some greasy fast food delivered right to my door. And a nap.

So, four things.

I lived on the north side of Norman. Far enough from the university campus to avoid the traffic on game days, and yet close enough to reach all the restaurants that call campus home. I measured most of the important things in my life by how close they were to my favorite food places. My office, which I was now no longer permitted to enter, was two blocks from a great Thai place. My house was equidistant between a fried chicken place and a fancy burger joint. Frankie and Dorian's apartment was walking distance from a 24/7 donut shop that sold a donut stuffed with chocolate and hazelnut cream.

My house was in a newer part of town, built within the last quarter century, making it the fancy part of town. I think. It was a house, and I lived in it. I even owned it, thanks to an inheritance from my father. It had two bedrooms, two bathrooms, a roof. One of those creepy attic crawlspaces I was a little too freaked out by to use. An office, where I spent most of my time. Standard, but not exceptional by any means. Housing was cheap in this area compared to a lot of other places. Perhaps the fact that there was a ten percent chance you could lose your home in a tornado any given year was what kept the cost of living so attractive to those not familiar with the insanity of our weather.

I pulled into the garage, fumbled my way inside through the dark, and headed for the shower, stripping as I went. It was honestly harder than I thought it would be. I got my arms stuck in the damn halter top, and I almost tripped on the fishnets.

"Why can't jeans and a baggy shirt be appropriate club

wear for women?" I grumbled as I unstuck my toe from a hole in the stockings I may or may not have accidentally ripped a little larger than it was intended to be. No big deal. They were going in the trash anyway.

A nap was rapidly nearing the top of my wish list. I could get some well-needed rest, have an unhealthy yet delicious lunch delivered after, and then ...

What, exactly? Wait for Benji to deliver the occasional report? Sit on the couch in my pajamas, twiddling my thumbs while Howell solved my Dust case?

The anger I'd felt earlier returned. I fumed while scrubbing layers of heavy makeup from my face in the shower. Dorian would be pissed if he knew I'd rubbed away all his hard work with my body wash instead of the super expensive facial cleanser he'd recommended based on my skin type and that I definitely did not pick up like he insisted.

Men. Can't live with them, can't get dressed for a night out without them.

So I fumed. And frankly, got downright pissed. I'd worked too hard on this Pixie Dust bullshit to have some clown with nice hair come in at the last minute. And Feldman's death was too intimate to be just a random murder. Someone, likely the Dust manufacturer or another close to him, was trying like hell to cover their tracks.

Which meant I must have been close to a breakthrough.

I finished my shower, bypassed the sweatpants and loose tank top waiting for me on my rumpled-up bed, and pulled out some jeans and one of my many plain black tees.

I may have had to turn in all the available paper files on the Dust ring to Howell, if they hadn't already been collected and sent his way, but I could still access the digital ones. At least until Ross got around to suspending my account privileges and locking me out of the system. If I was lucky, I still had an hour, maybe two, to digest the scans and reports of everything OKAPD had uncovered about Dust. There was a chance something in those files could help me investigate on my own.

I waited for my clunky APD-issue laptop to boot up. The thing was ancient, and I had been due for an upgrade for two years now, but our budget never seemed to allow for one—a heavy downside to functioning so far out of the public eye.

I waited, pressing my bare feet into a little wooden foot massager I kept on the floor under my desk. My feet ached terribly from the boots I'd worn to the club. I wasn't used to wearing anything with a heel, and those things had been clunky and uncomfortable. When I finally got to the login screen for OKAPD's database, I quickly entered my credentials and waited while it thought about admitting me.

And then I got the popup I was desperately hoping not to get:

'Access Denied. Account Under Lockdown.'

"Dammit, Ross."

Why I'd thought for even a moment he might not have already locked my account was beyond me. He'd probably locked it before I left the building.

All I could do now was check emails, and even those were monitored. No way Benji could send any files to me without Ross catching him.

I shut the laptop down and stared at the black screen for a moment.

There was only one thing left to do. And there was a good chance it wouldn't work. Ross could be on my ass extending my suspension before I realized it.

But I would have to give it a try anyway.

If Feldman was murdered by someone working closely

with the Dust manufacturer, then I needed to act now. I didn't trust anyone, not even Howell and his special credentials, to get this dealt with before the trail went cold.

My nap and fast food would have to wait. I wasn't giving up so easily.

FOUR

y little Blackbird was getting some mileage on
her today.

I rode back up to Bricktown. I even parked
in the same parking garage, though it was emptier in the daytime. I got a spot on the second floor, rather than the third, and I gave the old girl a little pat on the seat before locking my helmet away. There were a couple of black sedans parked in the fire zone across the street, right in front of Club 405, and a police officer paced the sidewalk out front. I didn't recognize him, which meant he was either OKAPD from another district, which was unlikely given how well staffed our office was, or he wasn't an APD officer at all. At first glance and to the untrained eye, OKAPD officers looked just like regular police officers. Even on second glance, many of them still did.

I watched him for a moment, feigning looking at my cell and checking the surrounding street signs as if to get my bearings. If he noticed me, he shrugged my appearance off as another pedestrian searching for their next stop.

Meanwhile, I channeled just a touch of the arcane energy within me to do a quick aura check.

This will come as no surprise to anyone that has done any sort of dabbling in the arcane forces, but people have auras. Many objects have auras, too. A knife used to commit murders, especially multiple ones, will have an aura. A necklace received from a loved one and worn for many years will develop an aura.

Arcane objects and people with arcane talent have bigger, brighter auras.

If you have the skill, it's a very simple task to do an aura check. It's like a quick arcane blink.

Blink, you see the auras. Blink again, and they're gone.

Sustaining that aura check into an aura search was an entirely different matter. That felt more like a staring contest, where each passing second drained you of arcane energy and which left you fatigued and could even make you sick. I made the mistake of holding an aura check for too long once and gave myself a nosebleed that lasted for over an hour. I had to be admitted to the emergency room. It wasn't a mistake I wanted to make again.

So I blinked. And then I blinked again. Aura check on, aura check off.

There was nothing on the police officer across the way.

Well, not nothing. Nothing would have been terrifying. Anything with absolutely no aura would be a demon, a soul that had lost its aura in return for eternal life and a bad attitude. And one did not fuck with demons.

The officer had a minimal aura. Nothing fantastic. Nothing to indicate any kind of arcane talent or skill. A mundane police officer.

Interesting that Howell has mundane officers on the crime scene.

I didn't cross the street. Not just yet. Instead I continued down the road, heading for the nearest corner. There was a coffee shop there, and I spent a few moments inside. It could have been luck that a coffee shop was so close, but frankly they were dotted pretty regularly through Bricktown. If there hadn't been one on that particular corner, there would have been one only another block down.

Now armed with coffee, I crossed the street at the intersection and made my way down to Club 405. It wasn't even eight in the morning yet, so traffic in that part of town was light. I made it to the black sedans and started trudging up the walkway to Club 405's main entrance.

The officer immediately flagged me down. "You can't go up there, Miss. This is a crime scene."

I could just barely make out yellow tape billowing slightly in the breeze across the open door on the side of the building.

"I know," I answered brightly. "I'm shadowing Detective Howell today. I brought him some coffee." I gave the officer an energetic smile and held up both hands, each one holding a paper cup filled with liquid energy. "Do you know how he takes it?"

"I'm going to need to see some ID," the officer said, approaching with a hand on his taser.

You'd really tase a woman holding two cups of coffee?

"Oh, right." I made as if to reach for a badge, then stopped, glancing at the coffees. I twisted my left side towards him. "It's there in my jacket pocket."

The officer reached, and I twisted away. "Oh, sorry. Wrong pocket." I chuckled. "That one's got the creams and sugars."

The officer rolled his eyes.

I twisted the opposite side towards him. "That pocket, pretty sure."

The officer just waved me on. "Howell's inside."

I gave him another energetic smile. "Thank you! I'm so excited for my first real crime scene!"

"Right," the officer said with a sardonic grin.

Once I got into the building, none of the other officers seemed to give me a second glance. It was, after all, the first guy's job to keep weirdos out of the building. If I was inside, it obviously meant I had shown proper credentials and passed his scrutiny.

If this didn't work, that poor officer was going to get a really stern talking to.

I found Howell standing in the archway separating the dance floor from the hallway leading to the bathrooms. The floor was littered with trash—napkins, several small plastic shot glasses, a few condom wrappers, and even a cheap bubblegum-pink wig. When Feldman's body was found and the police called, they must have cleared the building out, staff included. I took a quick look up to the plexiglass roof over the bar. The pink martini glass was still there, as was the champagne flute. And there were small dried spots of colored liquid that at one point had probably been mixed drinks. The whole place had lost its club appeal and looked just kind of grimy and gross in the harsh white fluorescent lights.

To be fair, the owner probably didn't have to deal with a murder investigation most days, giving his staff the opportunity to clean and get the place party-ready again.

I shook my head and sidestepped an overturned chair.

Howell was shuffling through a stack of photographs when I approached. His back was to me, and I held out the coffee in my left hand for him.

He took it without looking up. "Thanks."

I stared at the topmost photograph over Howell's shoulder. It showed Feldman's body as it must have been found at the crime scene. His hands were still cuffed around the toilet. And his eyes were looking straight up at the ceiling. I fought down a gag at the realization that his neck had been twisted clean around. Benjamin had said it was bad, but the photo was *bad*. "Anything I can help with, Detective Howell?"

Howell looked up in surprise. "I thought Ross was going to suspend you, Maxwell?"

"He did." I pulled out a handful of creamers and sugar packets and held them out. "Need any?"

"Then just what the hell are you doing here?" Howell asked.

"Asking if you need any help. I don't think Feldman's death was just a coincidence." I offered the mess of coffee condiments again, but Howell only stared at me. I shrugged and returned them to my pocket. "I was hoping to get another hour to look at the digital files before Ross locked my account, but I guess he wasn't planning on giving me so much as an inch to work with." I separated a slim yellow sweetener packet from the collection in my pocket and tore the top off with my teeth. Howell watched me pour the contents of the packet into my coffee through the hole in the lid. I pocketed the trash and gave the coffee cup a careful swirl. "Then I remembered you saying you would be at the crime scene all morning, and I thought maybe you might appreciate a little assistance."

Howell's face was unreadable. "You thought wrong, Maxwell. This is a crime scene. And do I need to remind you that you're still our only suspect?"

"So Feldman was murdered?" I took a sip of my coffee. "Not that I really had any doubts, with his head all spun around like that."

Howell glared. "Leave, Maxwell. Leave now, and I won't call Ross about this."

I raised my hands defensively. "I'm not here to cause trouble, I promise. I just think that you ought to know we're running out of time."

"What's that supposed to mean?"

"It means," I said, fumbling around for something plausible that might keep me from getting kicked out, "that I think whoever is behind Feldman's murder is doing some clean-up work. Meaning that we're close to busting them. I wouldn't be surprised if they're packing up their operation and getting ready to move it elsewhere. If we're too slow to get this figured out, they'll be gone by the time we move on them."

Howell's shoulders relaxed. "I had the same thought."

"I just want to catch this guy, so let me help." I shrugged. "Two heads are better than one and all that."

Howell considered for a moment. He sipped at his coffee, glancing down at the file in his hand. It was still open to the photo of Feldman's body. "I'm not with the OKAPD," he finally said. "I'm just a normie."

I nodded. "I figured." I motioned towards the street. "Your guy out there is a normie, too."

Howell returned the nod. "Everyone out here is. We're handling this as OKPD. As a favor to Ellis."

"Right. Keep the APD a secret from everyone not in the know."

"And to give the public some familiar faces to see when questions are asked about this death. And the relation to Pixie Dust, when that gets out."

"Dust is a danger to everyone, mundane or not." I shrugged again. "Tell them this was a drug-related murder, the public will buy it easy."

"Because it is a drug-related murder, right?" Howell asked.

"Oh, definitely." I relaxed a little. If Howell was asking questions, chances were good he wouldn't call Ross. "It's a drug murder in relation to a drug that seems to be manufactured as a narcotic and arcane-energy blend, which has been reported to cause some pretty insane side effects in its users."

"I saw the reports. Briefly. Some people are dying within minutes of ingesting Dust. Others are witnessed to be levitating or floating hours after using."

"Which is what gave it the nickname in the first place."

Howell nodded. "Peter Pan using Tinkerbell's pixie dust to give the Darlings the ability to fly," Howell said. "Clever, if it weren't so deadly."

"We still haven't figured out the pattern between who dies and who just gets to experience a new definition to 'having a great high', but I have a theory."

"Yeah?" Howell asked.

I sipped at my coffee again. "Promise you won't call Ross about my little visit?"

Howell tilted his head, scrutinizing me. "I won't call him *yet*."

"Fair enough." I sighed. "I think the ones dying were all Blanks."

"Blanks?"

I nodded. "Many mundane people have a small spark of some sort of arcane talent in them. It's what makes some people a little luckier than others, or makes someone particularly calming to be around."

"Or makes it so that they can fry eggs without ever breaking the yolks?"

I chuckled. "I guess, sure."

"Huh." Howell walked over to a table, and I followed him. "My grandmother always said we had a bit of the talent in the family. I thought it was just wishful thinking, or that it had diluted to nothing over the generations. But that woman fried eggs for breakfast every morning, and she never broke a single yolk in the eighty-five years she was here. I never knew how she did it."

I pulled out a chair with an annoying squeal on the polished cement floor and took a seat. "There you go. She wasn't as mundane as you thought."

"Alright, so then what about Blanks?"

"Blanks don't have a drop of arcane talent in them at all. Your guy outside is a Blank. He might be a great cop, but he'll never have those incredible hunches that break open cases or be the lucky guy that's in the right place at the right time to catch a murderer or stop a bank robbery."

"And what makes you think all the deaths related to using Dust are of Blanks?"

I shrugged. "I dunno. The only thing I can think is that their bodies can't handle the arcane energy in the drug, and it's killing them."

"And the others, the ones floating around?"

"Mundanes. They have a little bit of that energy already present, so the drug just amplifies them."

"And makes them fly?" Howell raised an eyebrow.

"I told you it was just a theory."

"It's better than the whole lot of nothing I had before." He finished off his coffee. "Does Ellis know about your theory?"

I snorted. "Ellis wouldn't give a damn about my theory on the sky being blue instead of piss yellow." Howell noted the bitterness to my tone with an amused tilt of his head, so I added meekly, "Not until I proved it, anyway."

"How can you prove it?"

"Short of asking a Blank to take some Dust and see if it kills them? I don't know if I can."

Howell set the file on the table between us. "I told you my nan had that weird trick with the egg yolks. But I have my own little trick, too. I'm pretty good at knowing when someone is bullshitting me."

I sighed. "I'm not bullshitting you, Howell. I promise."

Howell nodded. "I'm pretty sure you're not, too. And I could honestly use someone with a better grasp of the arcane and more knowledge of this case to help me out. I figured Ross would have given me someone, but I haven't heard anything yet."

"No one knows this case like I do," I said. "I'll be happy to help."

"Good." He sat, shuffling through the stack of photos once more. "What do you make of the symbol on Feldman's hand?"

"What symbol?"

Howell lifted a photo for me to inspect, and I took it. It was a close-up of Feldman's right hand, and there was an irregular and asymmetrical design drawn onto the back of his hand in red ink.

"I thought at first it was the club's stamp, but it doesn't seem like the right aesthetic."

I held up my own hand, back facing Howell. A faded, stylized 405 was stamped on my skin in black ink. "No, this is their stamp. I was here last night, remember?"

"So what do you think that is?" Howell asked with a nod at the photo in my hands.

"I don't know." I stared at it for a moment, trying to recall if I had seen the same symbol in any other files about the growing Dust ring. "It looks arcane, but not something I'm familiar with."

"An arcane symbol on the back of Feldman's hand? Did you notice it last night?"

I shook my head. "Feldman is left-handed. I noticed when he pulled the Dust from his pocket. So I focused on getting that hand cuffed first. The rest ..." I shrugged. "The rest just kind of happened too quick to notice something like that."

"Detective Howell?" A male officer appeared from the

hallway leading to the bathroom, stopping a respectful distance when he saw Howell and me in discussion. "The manager's got the cameras up for you."

Howell straightened. "Great, we'll be right there." He reached for the photo, but I pulled it back.

"Mind making me a sketch of this symbol on that little notebook you've got?"

Howell did, placing the photo beside his notebook and carefully copying the symbol with a handful of pen strokes. He used a fountain pen, of course. Bonus points for style. The ink was a professional black, though. I would have gone with a bright purple myself.

"Got some ideas on where you might be able to figure out what it means?" He tore the page from his notebook and passed it to me.

"Nope." I folded the paper in half and slipped it into my back pocket as I got to my feet. "But I'll think of something."

CHAPTER

FIVE

I followed Howell down the hall where Club 405's bathrooms were. The men's room was blocked with crime scene tape, and the officer that had called for Howell a moment ago was standing guard. I got a sick sensation in my stomach as we passed, and I couldn't help but stare at the yellow streamers crossed over the opening.

Is it my fault Feldman died? Could I have stopped it if I'd waited for Benjamin like I should have? Or would we both have been killed?

The women's bathroom was left without tape over the entrance, and I mentally gave the little wineglass decal beside the entrance the finger as I passed.

The third door I noted earlier that morning opened onto a small office that seemed to double as a janitor's closet. There were a few large push brooms and a couple of mop buckets in one corner. A crate full of various cleaners sat on the floor beside them, and a faint lemon scent filled the air. There were some metal lockers on the opposite wall, arranged in a two-by-two grid, and a familiar studded BMX helmet sat on top of them.

Another officer was waiting inside, standing next to a

desk cluttered in papers and video recording equipment. A balding middle-aged man sat in the only chair, which faced a dual monitor set up that had been split into four camera views. The footage was paused, and I saw two views of the dance floor, a third of the bar in the back, and one shot of the hallway. And in the last camera, frozen in greyscale, was the back of Feldman's spiked head.

The balding man, the manager I assumed, looked up as Howell and I entered. He looked panicked and afraid. Not unreasonable for someone who'd had a murder in his club just a few hours before.

I pointed at the BMX helmet. "You guys employ a full-time DJ? I assumed he was a gig guy."

The manager seemed surprised by the question. "W-we take turns wearing the helmet. Most of the DJ shows are on automatic timers. Everything is already synced to the lights."

"So last night the DJ was just faking it?" I was surprised. He was putting on a good show from what I remembered seeing.

"I was in the helmet last night—I do all my own mixing. Only my light shows are automatic."

Now I was really surprised. "You were the DJ last night?"

The manager looked from me to Howell. "I'm sorry, but what does this have to do with the death of that man?"

Howell gave me a sideways glance, and I shook my head slightly.

"It has nothing to do with it. My partner here is just asking out of ill-timed curiosity." Howell motioned towards the monitors. "You have the footage of the deceased ready?"

"Y-yes. I was able to retrace his entire visit to the club last night based on when the call to the authorities first went out and the club was emptied."

"He came in about two hours before this shot was captured," the officer explained. He addressed Howell alone, ignoring me completely. I guessed I deserved that for asking about DJing during a murder investigation. "He bought a few drinks at the bar, went back to the bathrooms briefly, and then returned and was on the dance floor for most of his time here. He tried dancing with a few people, most of whom were uninterested." The officer nodded to the manager, who hit a button on the keyboard. "And then this woman approached him."

Feldman stepped further into the camera view, and guess which APD detective was trailing behind him? The manager paused the recording again, and I got a nice look at the back half of my body. My hair looked great. My ass looked better.

The officer gave the manager another nod, and he hit a second button on the keyboard. This one played the footage at about five times the speed. "She followed him into the bathroom and is seen exiting a few minutes later."

"Is this the one that ... did it?" the manager asked Howell.

On the screen, I exited the bathroom and disappeared from the camera's view.

Howell sighed. "No. That's my partner here. Undercover."

I waved at the manager. "Hi." I pointed at Howell. "I'm his partner."

"Oh." The manager's face screwed up. "But no one else entered the bathroom until the police showed up."

As if on cue, three officers appeared in one of the dance floor camera views. The manager paused the recording, then played it forward at regular speed. I recognized the officer on point as Benji, and pointed him out to Howell. Howell nodded.

Benji and the other two officers crossed the dance floor, startling several of the dancers. Many filed out very quietly. The tables, which had been full when I left, quickly emptied when those seated realized the party might be ending a bit early.

I thought I recognized the other two officers with Benjamin. Or I could at least narrow them down to three or so of my coworkers. "Did you get to talk with all three of them, Howell?"

"Yeah. All said the same thing. Officer Jackson led them in, they made straight for the suspect, and when they entered the bathroom they found him deceased."

The officers appeared on the hallway camera, approaching the men's room in a V shape. They flanked the doorway, and after a brief hesitation Benji stormed in. The other two officers followed him, and then all three appeared again only seconds later. Benjamin was already calling in on his walkie while the other two made to seal the club's exit. The lights came up on the dance floor, and those who had missed the police entrance froze in surprise. I was watching with interest, and it took me a second to realize the manager had paused the recording again.

"After that, more officers arrived and began questioning those present. No one claims to have seen anything," the officer said. He was staring at me with an accusatory look even though his words were directed at Howell.

"There aren't cameras in the bathroom," the manager said. "F-for obvious reasons. But that's the only way in or out." He rubbed at his bald spot. "Anyone going in or coming out would have shown up on this camera."

"Shit," I muttered, "that can't be all of it. Maybe someone was waiting for Feldman inside the bathroom?"

But the bathroom had been empty. I remembered as much, and I had already told Howell the same.

"I thought you said you ran into someone in the hall on your way out, Maxwell?" Howell asked.

"I did. Big guy. Didn't really get a good look at him."

Howell nodded at the manager. "Rewind it and replay, please?"

The manager backed the recording up with a button press. Benji and the others backtracked first to the bathroom, and then across the dance floor. I appeared in the entrance a moment later, walking backwards until I reached the bathroom as well.

"Play it from here," I said. I pointed at the bottom corner of the camera's view. "He should show up right here, right as I'm about to leave the hallway."

The manager played it. On the screen, I walked down the hallway, closer to the camera, though it was angled above me. You could see my face clearly, even in the greyscale. Right down to the shadow forming around my eye.

I touched my eye. It hurt like hell. And it had been a bitch to cover up. Makeup alone hadn't done the trick. I'd had to glamor it up with a touch of arcane energy. It was uncomfortable, and the constant drain on my body from maintaining the glamor would tire me out after a few hours. I had no idea how long a black eye would last, and I cursed myself for not dodging Feldman's hair spike.

Camera Ava turned the small corner around the archway and disappeared from the hall cam's sight. At the same time, I appeared on one of the videos showing the dance floor, coming through that same archway.

Howell shook his head. "No one was there."

"There was someone there," I insisted. "Back it up again and play it slower."

"Maxwell, there was no one there." Howell sighed. "Look, I believe you when you say Feldman was still alive when you left him, but ..." He paused for a second, looking at the camera feed. "You'd just been in an altercation with the deceased. When I saw you this morning, you had a black eye. No amount of makeup can cover it up—your face is still bruised to hell."

Ouch. Guess I need to work on my glamor skills.

"Are you suggesting that I imagined it? That the hit to my head or the black eye made me think someone was there?"

Howell shrugged. "It's possible."

I pulled him away from the officer and the manager. "Howell, I bumped into someone." I kept my voice low, glancing up at the officer and the club's manager. They were both watching the screens intently. "I didn't just see them. I felt them."

Howell frowned, like he didn't understand the point I was trying to make.

I sighed. "It's easy enough for someone with a good amount of arcane talent to hide themselves from cameras. But I know what I saw. And what I felt."

"You think someone like you killed Feldman?"

Someone like me?

"If you mean someone with arcane abilities, then yes. But they would have to be stronger than me. I don't have enough skill with that kind of working to hide myself from cameras."

"Detective."

Howell and I both looked up. The officer was looking at Howell, of course. I was just some nobody to the officers here. Definitely not a fellow officer that happened to be suspended at the moment.

"There's something there," the officer said, nodding at the monitors.

We both approached, and the manager pointed at the

very bottom corner of the video. It was paused, and camera Ava was just stepping over the threshold and was two, perhaps three frames away from walking out of the view frame. My right hand was raised, mouth opened slightly, and I was leaning away from the wall.

Classic Midwestern 'Ope, sorry, didn't see you there' motion.

And there was a shadow on the wall of the archway. It was indistinct, but it was definitely there.

The officer pointed to another view frame, this one of the dance floor where the camera was pointed at the archway. The view was partially obstructed by a raised hand on the dance floor, and by the archway itself, but you could see one of my legs from knee to thigh, my right elbow and part of my forearm, and my right shoulder on up. The entire left side of my body was obscured by the archway.

And there was the shadow again. Indistinct, not entirely human shaped, and clearly not a person. But the officer was right. Something was there.

"I'm not sure what it is. Maybe just a shadow caused by the light show?" The manager shrugged.

Howell nodded. "I'm sure that's all it is. But I'd like to have someone in our lab take a closer look, if you don't mind."

I crossed my arms, glaring at Howell.

The manager nodded. "Sure, I'll get this stuff downloaded for you right away."

Howell turned and left the office, taking me by the elbow as he went.

I pulled my elbow from his grip and followed him silently until we were back in the club's main room. "Detective Howell—"

Howell turned on his heel, giving me a very sincere look. "I believe you."

That stopped me. "You do?"

"Yeah." Howell nodded. "I've seen some shit, and I know about some of the things people like you can do from what Ellis has told me over the years."

That phrase again.

Howell pointed back at the office. "That shadow ... man ... thing is likely the killer. And I don't know a damned thing about how to chase down an arcane user." He gave me a stern look. "You want to help? Then help me figure out how we can track that thing down."

My shoulders relaxed some, and I took a deep breath. "An arcane user knew Feldman was at the club, watched us go back to the bathrooms, then slipped past me to kill him. Maybe someone saw something before he got inside the club?"

Howell crossed his arms. "My first thought would be to question the bouncer. Anyone entering the club would have gone right by him. But he hasn't been heard from since the club was evacuated."

I bit my lip.

Could the bouncer be involved somehow, or has he just been out of reach for some reason?

My phone rang, startling me. Frankie's name showed up on the caller ID. Or, to be more accurate, Frankie's Dungeons and Dragons character name with a bunch of music notes and lutes to either side of it. He saved his number in my phone, not me. I'd just been too lazy to change it.

"I need to answer this." I walked several steps away, not waiting for Howell's response.

"Please tell me you have some good news for me, Frankie."

"Did you know you have some expired pepperoni slices in your fridge?" Frankie's voice was muffled, as if he were speaking around a mouthful of food.

"Are you raiding my pantry?"

"It's not really raiding if there's not much in there."

"How did you get into my house?"

"Please, I know you keep the door from the garage to the house unlocked. And I guessed you were too lazy to change the garage code from the default one-two-three-four."

He was right. I sighed. "Do you have those reports for me?"

"Yup. I'm going to finish off this tube of summer sausage and leave it in your office." I heard the sound of plastic ripping. "Since *someone* was supposed to have tacos for me and flaked."

"I'm sorry, I'm working a murder investigation," I said sarcastically.

"Anyone I know? That bitch at the nail salon who tried to say pastel green wasn't a good color on me?" I heard him biting into something, and his next words were muffled again. "I'm Mexican. Everything looks fabulous on me."

I rolled my eyes. "I'll take a look at your reports when I can, but can you give me the short version?"

"The Dust you brought me this morning is almost an identical match to the last vial I tested. The differences are minimal, and are likely due to them being different production batches. Which means someone is actually doing a really great job of maintaining quality."

"Odd, considering it's killing people so quickly."

Frankie paused, then asked, "Have you considered the idea that it's designed to do exactly that?"

I had not.

"And there was something else I noticed that was super-interesting."

"Yeah?"

"The methamphetamine in this Dust stuff you gave me that has a twenty percent D-isomer concentration."

I sighed. "I don't know what that means, Frankie."

"It means someone is being very careful to make this drug exactly the way they want it to be. A twenty percent D-isomer concentration doesn't usually just happen."

"Why is the isomer thing important? In a drug, I mean."

Now Frankie sighed. "Alright, put your hands up, palms out."

I sandwiched the phone between my cheek and shoulder and did as he said. "Okay."

"Your right hand is a mirror of your left, yes?"

I snorted. "Well, yeah." I touched my thumbs together. "All my little fingers match up."

"But they don't line up when superimposed, right?"

"You mean when I put one hand on top of the other? Not unless I've got two left hands."

Frankie yawned in my ear. "So even though they're mirrors of each other, would you say they're the same?"

I grabbed the phone again and shook my head. "No. One's a left hand and the other is a right hand."

"Correct."

"And this is like the isomer thing?"

"Correct again."

"Aaand, I'm supposed to do what with this information?"

"Isomers don't always act like their partner. Only the D-isomer of methamphetamine is the icky, illegal one. The L-isomer is sold in over-the-counter medicines and can be used to treat Parkinsons."

"So, someone is trying very hard to make this drug only twenty percent illegal?"

Frankie snorted. "It sounds more like someone is

controlling the concentrations of everything in this Dust stuff down to like, a pharmaceutical grade."

"Huh."

"I wouldn't have caught the isomer thing normally. I just happened to add the test to the queue as an afterthought." He paused, then added, "You're welcome."

"What about the arcane component? Can you tell how it's bound into the drug?"

Frankie snorted again. "No. That's your area, honey. Not mine."

Technically true, but I knew next to nothing about mixing the arcane with the mundane. It was common practice for herbal arcanists, but my talents had always been in conjurations. Fireballs and energy blasts, not poultices and pain amulets.

I rubbed at a spot above my eyebrow. I could feel a headache coming on. "Thanks, bitch."

"Later, ho."

Frankie hung up, and I turned to see Howell staring at me. Feldman's file was open in his hands again.

"You have good news?"

I shook my head. "Not really. But I have a new theory."

"Yeah?" Howell raised an eyebrow. "The Blanks one no good?"

"Actually, consider it an amendment to that." I bit my lip, thinking. "What if Dust is designed to target and kill Blanks? That it's not an accident that they're the ones dying?"

"If they are indeed the ones dying," Howell corrected. But he nodded. "A kind of hate crime, then? Against people with no arcane ability?"

I nodded.

Howell looked down at the file in his hands, shuffling through a few pages. "This says you were led to Feldman by another dealer. One you were able to get a possession conviction on. Do you think he might know more than he's already shared?"

"It's worth checking out."

I knew exactly which dealer he meant. And I knew exactly where I could find him.

CHAPTER

SIX

Ivan "the Iron" Tooms, so named for reasons that I'm sure were related to his multiple run-ins with APD and our inability to get a conviction on him, lived in a rundown single wide trailer just north of central Norman, Oklahoma. Despite multiple arrests for drug and weapon possession, and several warnings for violating the thin veil of secrecy between the mundane and arcane worlds by staging episodes of self-immolation to frighten away door-to-door salesmen, Tooms had yet to see the inside of a courtroom. Until I bagged him six months ago in my first arrest in relation to Dust.

It was a solid case. He was found with a vial of Dust on him, within a school zone, and was arrested by yours truly after I went undercover as a student.

One of the earliest victims of Dust was a high schooler, and I was convinced someone close to the school was dealing directly to the students.

Not only was Tooms employed as a maintenance worker and often took jobs that brought him into the school, but his rundown home was in a quaint trailer park just across the street from the high school.

His conviction brought him no jail time, despite the evidence stacked against him. He pleaded guilty on a misdemeanor charge and accepted probation and a year of house arrest and gave us three names of other prolific Dust dealers in the Norman and OKC metro area. One of those names was a dud. The guy was a dealer, but not of Dust. He was rolled over to NPD and dealt with by their drug force.

The second name was Feldman.

The third name was not really a name at all, and had been rolling around in the back of my mind ever since Tooms first uttered it.

I rode back to Norman on my Blackbird. Howell followed behind in his nondescript black sedan with obvious state police plates. I couldn't quite remember where in the maze of the trailer park Tooms's house was, so I rolled slowly through the first few streets and looked for the ugliest, most rundown one.

People often assumed that anyone living in any kind of prefabricated house was going to have questionable home maintenance skills or simply didn't care about their house. Most of the time, that thinking was incorrect at best. Many of the houses in the neighborhood I passed had nicer front gardens than I did, and more than a couple of them had a lovely wind chime hanging from an eave or a cute yard sign. A woman in capris and a summery blouse and sun hat lounged on a chaise on her large porch with a tiny dog in her lap. The dog's ears perked up as I passed, but neither pet nor owner made any move from their sunny spot.

Tooms's house was very much unlike the rest in his neighborhood. When it came to him, that unfair and cruel stereotype was fairly accurate, which made picking his home out a fairly simple task. The siding was an ugly yellow stained with the red clay of Oklahoma's soil. It could have used a power wash maybe five years ago. The corner of the roof sagged noticeably, and there was an air of general neglect over the place. The car was a garage fixer-upper, but since there was no garage, it took up residence in the driveway. And it looked like it hadn't been worked on in some time. It was the kind of house that, in areas with homeowners' associations, would receive the brunt of complaints and get the blame for poor property values in the neighborhood.

I doubled back, parking the Blackbird by the main entrance right next to Howell's sedan. Howell was waiting for me, leaning against the back of the sedan on his arms. He'd taken off his suit jacket and stowed it away in the back seat. He seemed more relaxed without the jacket, and the pale blue of the button-up shirt complemented his skin tone and hair color nicely.

"What do you know about Tooms, Howell?" I asked, locking my helmet into the hard-shell tail bag and pocketing the keys.

"I know you guys have been hounding him for a couple of years," Howell said. He flicked open a pair of sunglasses in a quick and fluid motion and slipped them on. I couldn't tell if they were knock-offs or legit, but they looked good on him.

"He's a real piece of shit," I said bluntly. "But we've only had the one conviction on him."

"Is he a piece of shit because you can't snag him, or is he a piece of shit that you can't seem to snag?"

"He's just a piece of shit."

"And yet he gave you Feldman," Howell said.

"To save himself. He was going to get some real jail time." I kicked a piece of loose gravel. "And now Feldman is gone. And I'm right back to hounding Tooms."

We came up on a corner, and Tooms's house came into view. Howell pointed at the rundown trailer, picking it out easily from the better-kept ones surrounding it. I nodded, and our footsteps fell into sync as we approached.

"Do you think Tooms has anything else left to tell us?" Howell asked.

"I really hope so."

There were two dark green city waste cans at the side of the house closest to the street and a rusted push mower chained to the front steps. Aside from those few things and the rusted car, which I now noted had three tires and a cinderblock, Tooms kept nothing else out around his house. There were no potted plants, no yard signs, not even a welcome mat in front of the door. Or even a *get the hell off my porch* mat. I knocked on the storm door, which rattled in the frame. The vinyl siding needed replacing. There were holes from what might have been good-sized hail, and several cracks and splits from age. The wood porch was beginning to rot, and it creaked unpleasantly underfoot.

"Want me to go around to the back?" Howell asked.

"Nah, he's not going to run."

I knocked again, harder, and muffled sounds of movement came through the cheap aluminum door.

Tooms opened the door, glaring at me through the thin glass that separated us. "Oh great, it's you."

"Morning, Tooms. Mind if I come in?" I opened the storm door before he could answer and let myself and Howell in.

"Like I have a choice." Tooms stepped back to let us through. "What brings you here, Detective? Want to try your hand at another conviction?" Tooms laughed and collapsed into a dirty recliner. His laugh was a phlegmy smoker's laugh, and the whole place stank of cigarette smoke. There was also the lingering smell of weed and citrusy cleaners.

"I might be, Tooms. You make so many stupid choices

in life. One of them is bound to come back and bite you in the ass."

"And yet here I am. Serving my sentence in the comfort of my own home instead of on the inside of a prison cell." Tooms pulled a crumpled red and white package from his breast pocket and lit a fresh cigarette, then shoved the pack away again. "Must drive you nuts, Detective."

"You been smoking pot, Tooms?" Howell asked. "Aren't you a little too close to the school to be in possession of something like that?"

Tooms gave Howell a glare, cigarette dangling limply from his lips. "I've got a medical card for it. And my probation officer helped me measure out the distance. As long as I smoke in my bedroom, I'm fine."

"What's the medical card for, Tooms?" I squinted at him. "You get headaches? Ask Dr. Feel Good to help you out?"

"Insomnia and night terrors, actually." Tooms tapped some ash off his cigarette and into a nearby ashtray. "A side effect of the Dust I was using last year. I did a sleep study and everything. My probation officer knows all about it."

Interesting.

"Okay, so maybe you're not doing anything with illegal substances," I said with a shrug. I took a look around his living room. I had to give it to him, Tooms kept a clean house. Everything was old and worn down, and there was the undeniable stain from years of smoke residue. But the place was tidy. The floors had recently been vacuumed, and there wasn't even a thin layer of dust on the TV stand. Which was more than I could say for my own house.

"What about murder, though, Tooms?" I asked, settling my gaze on him again.

Tooms raised an eyebrow at me mid-drag. "What?" The

question came out with a puff of smoke, and I waved it away.

"You gave me three names to get this sweet setup you've got." I counted them on my fingers for him to see. "Pickard wasn't a Dust dealer. So that one was useless to me."

Tooms leaned forward, pointing at me with the fingers clutching his cigarette. "I didn't say all of them would be Dust dealers. He was a dealer, and you wanted names."

I nodded. "I'll give you that, Tooms. Pickard was arrested."

"And you told the detective here about Feldman," Howell added.

Tooms leaned forward more, sitting on the edge of his seat now. "What more do you want from me about him? Roggie deals Dust. I told you where he likes to hang. If you haven't moved on him, that's on you."

"He's dead, Tooms."

Tooms fell back into his recliner. "Roggie's dead?"

I nodded. "He was murdered earlier today. So I need to know if you told anyone he was about to get snagged."

"What? No." Tooms shook his head. "You think I can just walk up to those guys and show my face? I don't even know where to look for them, but you can bet they'd beat the shit out of me on sight. Or worse, kill me." Tooms took a deep pull on his cigarette. His hands were shaking as he stamped it out. "Fuck."

"Did you tell anyone that you made a deal?" Howell asked.

Tooms looked from Howell to me. "Is your friend here an idiot?" He pulled another cigarette out of his pocket. "You want to know who I talked to about Roger Feldman?" He pointed at me. "You. You and the rest of your damned goon squad." He lit the cigarette and motioned to the door as he took another deep inhale. He blew the smoke out in a long stream, aiming it politely away from us. "I don't know why I'm still talking to you. You can't interrogate me without my lawyer. Please leave. I just finished work and I could use some sleep."

"This ain't an interrogation, Tooms," Howell said. "Think of it as you giving us a bit of help to find out who killed Feldman."

Tooms shook his head. "I've got no idea."

"Then tell me more about that third name you gave me," I said. "Tell me more about Mr. Hook."

Howell snorted, but Tooms and I kept our eyes locked on each other.

Tooms looked away first. "I don't know anything about him. Just that he's the one running things."

Howell chuckled. "Now I know I haven't had much time to catch up on this case, Maxwell. But I hope you're not saying the big mastermind behind Pixie Dust calls himself Mr. Hook? As in Captain Hook?" He gave me a lopsided grin. "I think I would have noticed a mention of that."

"There's no mention of it in the files, Howell," I said. "Ross insisted on keeping it out of any file or in any report to the media. To keep our knowledge of him as low-key as possible."

Tooms was staring in the middle distance, his cigarette close to his mouth. "It was the name he ended up with, not the one he asked for. Can't make a heavy drug like Dust and be called Peter Pan, can you?"

"What do you know about him, Tooms?" I asked again.

Tooms shook his head. "Nothing. Never met him. Never seen him."

"You've never heard anything about him? Nothing more than his name?"

Tooms hesitated.

"Come on, man." I squatted, bringing myself closer to his eye level. "Just give me whatever you can. I've got a dead dealer and nothing to get me closer to solving this one."

Tooms polished off his second cigarette in one final, slow drag. He held his breath for a moment, eyes squinting at me. "I don't know if it will help." He let the smoke out in a long exhale, blowing it off to the side again. "But I heard the guy is pretty weird. That he can do some crazy shit. You think my little burning stunts are bad?" Tooms shook his head, smashing the filter of his smoke into the ashtray. "I've apparently got nothing on this guy."

"What kind of crazy shit?" I asked.

"The kind of shit that you've been told isn't possible, even for people like us. He can walk through walls. Make himself disappear. Turn himself into animals." Tooms reached for the pack of cigarettes in his shirt pocket, but crumpled the package and dropped it into the ashtray. "Sounds like the kind of guy I really don't want to fuck with. And the accent just makes him a little more intimidating."

"Accent?"

"Yeah." Tooms nodded. "One of them fancy English accents. Makes him sound real smart. And real dangerous."

I thought about telling Tooms that anyone that can properly pronounce *rutabaga* probably sounds real smart to a Midwestern hick like him, but all I could manage was a surprised "Huh."

Tooms stood, and I stood with him. "I really don't have anything else, and I'm out of smokes. I need to get some sleep."

I nodded, motioning for Howell to lead the way back to the door. "Alright, Tooms. If this leads to anything helpful, I'll be sure to drop your name with your parole officer."

We saw ourselves out. Tooms shut the door behind us, and Howell and I hesitated on the sagging porch.

"So, this Mr. Hook guy can do magic? We knew that already."

"Now we know he's more powerful than we thought. Walking through walls is definitely not possible, but a well-timed transportation spell can make it look like you're walking through a wall. And body manipulation isn't easy. It's not something I can do, that's for sure."

"And the disappearance act?"

I took the steps down slowly. "Like I said earlier, the process is simple. It just takes a lot of power."

Howell put a hand on my shoulder. It was a cautious touch, and I stopped on the bottom step.

"You hear that?" he asked.

I listened.

There was a rattling, like a spray paint can, followed by the hiss of propellant. The sound was close, perhaps just around the corner of the house.

"Think someone's doing a little craft project?" I whispered.

"On the side of Tooms's house?" Howell descended the last steps, going around me. "I'll go around the long way. You take front."

"I don't have a gun," I said in a loud whisper.

"So use your special talents, Miss APD."

I took a stance on the corner of the house and waited for Howell to disappear around the far side. A quick peek was enough to see that the tagger wasn't on the side of the house facing the street, which made sense. That meant Howell would startle the tagger from his job and send him my way.

I sighed and shook my arms.

"Stop! Hands up!" Howell's voice was loud in the still morning air.

There was a clatter of metal and the sound of scuffling. I waited, listening.

There was an eerie sensation of static in the air and the brief tang of ozone quickly followed by a muffled explosion. It was almost like a soft sonic boom. Or the sound one of those large plastic toy guns makes when it launches off a big foam ball.

And then a curse from Howell and the sound of sliding gravel.

Hurried footsteps came closer, and I stepped out from around the corner of the house, both hands raised.

The kid was wearing a maroon hoodie and a slim backpack. All I could see of his face were large, frightened eyes before he raised his hands to launch another blast of arcane energy at me.

It rebounded off the shield I'd cast and hit him square in the chest, knocking him back into the two green trash cans. All three, cans and kid alike, spilled to the gravel.

"What the hell is going on out here?" Tooms had followed us outside and stood on the porch. Seeing how much it sagged under his weight made me wish I hadn't dared stand on it.

"Just some kid playing with spray paint. You can press charges if you want." I knelt and hauled the kid up by his hoodie, only to be surprised that *he* was actually a *she*. A grey beanie covered her hair, and the baggie hoodie hid her figure, but there was no mistaking it. "Come on, up you get."

Howell limped around the corner. His nice blue shirt was covered in dirt and grass. "Where were you, Maxwell?" He tossed me a pair of cuffs, and I slipped them easily over the girl's slim wrists.

"I was waiting for the chance to use my special talents, Mr. FBI." I passed the backpack to Howell, and he rummaged through the contents.

I took a moment to pat the girl down. No wallet on her. Nothing whatsoever in her pockets, as a matter of fact.

Howell sighed, holding the bag open so I could see two cans of red spray paint. "Got an ID over there?"

"Nah, you?"

Howell shook his head.

Tooms rushed down the stairs and ran past Howell and me. I heard his slippered feet sliding on the gravel and then crunching on dry grass. "What the hell is this?"

Howell took the teen by the elbow. "I'll walk her to the car. You should take a look at the graffito."

"Ooh, *graffito*," I mocked. I did my best Dowager Countess of Grantham impersonation. "How sophisticated."

"Shut up and go look, Maxwell."

Tooms was staring at the side of his house when I came up to him. "Who's going to pay for this to be cleaned off?"

The spray paint was already dry in most places, and drying quickly in the others. And the symbol was the same that had been drawn on the back of Feldman's hand. I took the folded slip of paper Howell had made for me earlier and compared the two designs. They were an exact match. We must have heard the tagger as she made her final few strokes. Where the red paint ran down the dirty and broken siding it looked an awful lot like blood.

I took out my cell phone and snapped a quick photo.

"I wouldn't wait to have it cleaned by someone else. I would get this cleaned off now."

SEVEN

We took Howell's sedan back to the Norman Police Department. I left my Blackbird where I'd parked it, though I gave the old gal a quick pat and a promise to come right back for her. Howell had the girl in the back seat, and I spent the short drive from Tooms's neighborhood to the police station staring at her reflection in my side mirror and trying to get a read on her. An aura check had come back with what little I already knew. The girl had arcane talent. A good amount, to be precise. Enough that she could be dangerous if she wanted to be.

"You broke my sunglasses with that little stunt of yours, kid," Howell said.

The girl said nothing.

"I'll buy you some new ones, you baby." I adjusted the thermostat. It was one of those fancy dual ones, and I made my side just a touch warmer than Howell's, mostly because I could.

"What the hell was that back there, Maxwell?" Howell asked me. His question was for me, but his eyes darted from the road in front of him to the rearview mirror, where I'm sure he was staring at the girl just as I was.

"Simple arcane energy blast. Channel enough energy and you can send it shooting out in a fixed direction," I answered.

The girl behind me made no indication she had heard either of us.

"Felt like I was hit with a beanbag gun."

That made her smirk.

"You may as well have been. A more powerful hit could have broken some ribs. Sent you to the hospital." I turned in my seat and drew the girl's attention. "And that kind of attack is what gets you stripped and censored for life."

The girl rolled her eyes at that.

"What's that mean?" Howell asked.

"If you're found guilty of something truly dangerous, your powers can be taken from you—stripped—and you'll be blacklisted from arcane-only establishments." I sat back in my seat. They were leather, with heat. It felt pretty nice.

"So you lose your special powers and your country-club membership?"

I shook my head. "You don't understand. For a lot of us, our talents are a huge part of our identity. Or our entire identity. Our community is the only one we feel safe and understood in. To lose that ..." I crossed my arms, looking at the girl's reflection again. "It drives some people insane."

The girl shifted uncomfortably. Howell did too, actually.

"You got a name, kid?"

Her discomfort instantly vanished, and she lifted her chin and stared into middle space.

I closed my eyes. "I'm sure we'll figure it out as soon as the fingerprints come back."

Howell seemed well known and well liked by the officers

at the Norman PD. I recognized a few of them from various APD run-ins. The officer that had let me into the club just a couple of hours ago was also there, and I gave him a smile as I followed Howell with the tagger's arm in my grip.

We were given an interrogation room and a fingerprint kit. Howell took the print himself. He was gentle with the young lady, even offering her an orange soda from their vending machine. She refused.

A half hour later I returned with a patrol officer to Tooms's neighborhood to fetch my bike. It had felt weird leaving it there, and weirder sitting in the passenger seat of a patrol car. Not that I was accustomed to sitting in the back seat, or anything. By the time I made it back to the interrogation room, Howell was already waiting with our tagger's name.

"Detective Maxwell, meet Virginia Vanderkamp." He waved a thin file at me before dropping it onto the table he and the girl sat at. "Just turned eighteen, meaning we don't have to call her parents just yet. Has been caught doing a few petty crimes. Seems she has sticky fingers and a love of vandalism."

The girl winced. "I prefer Ginny."

Ginny had taken off her beanie, and it was plain to see why she had worn it in the first place. Her hair had been bleached and dyed a shocking pink, then plaited into two tight French braids that ended at chin length. Dark roots were already growing out, but the rest of her hair was easily identifiable. And cool as hell. I had a brief vision of a similar look I had once rocked, though mine had come with a velvet choker and heavy pink and black smoky eyeshadow.

Ah, to be young again.

"Alright, Ginny," I started, taking a seat beside Howell. "What can you tell me about that symbol you were painting on that house?"

Ginny crossed her arms. Howell had uncuffed her. "Am I under arrest?"

Howell shrugged. "You were caught vandalizing private property. And you attacked two officers."

Ginny's expression shifted. She looked worried.

I pulled a red package from my jacket and tore it open. "Twizzler?" I offered the package to Ginny, who shook her head. I shrugged and took one for myself, biting off the end with relish. It was a little stale, but I hadn't eaten since stealing that bite of Frankie's cold ramen, and I was hungry.

"What is this, the Good Cop, Bad Cop routine?"

"More like the Cool Cop, Boring Cop." I propped my feet up on the table, ripping another bite off of my licorice. "I'll let you figure out which is which."

Ginny rolled her eyes. Howell crossed his arms and gave me an annoyed look.

"Alright, let me be honest with you, Ginny." I sat up, taking my feet from the table and giving her a sincere look. "That symbol you painted on that house was found on a dead man this morning."

"Maxwell," Howell warned.

I raised a hand to quiet him. "I don't think you just came up with that symbol all on your own and picked that particular house out of all the houses in this town to paint that symbol on."

Ginny bit her lip.

"I'm guessing someone asked you to go to that house and showed you the symbol to paint on it. I'm even going to guess that you have no idea what that symbol means."

Ginny shook her head.

I pressed further. "And now you're stuck in the middle of a murder investigation. You could be considered an accomplice. You could be tried for murder, too."

Beside me, Howell shifted but said nothing.

Ginny's face reddened. "I didn't do anything but tag some house, okay?" She was fighting back tears. "I don't know anything about a murder."

I shrugged. "I'm sure that's true, but it doesn't change the fact that painting that symbol has tied you to it. We believe you, but with your record ..." I let the rest of my words hang unspoken.

Ginny was crying very quietly. And I felt like a massive asshole.

Howell shifted forward. "I don't want you to be scared. If you can give us the name of the person that told you to do this, it'll be a lot easier to get your involvement cleared up."

"I don't know his name," Ginny said, wiping at her face. There was dried spray paint on the tip of her forefinger. "He came up to me after school yesterday. He knew my name. Knew my record. He said he'd give me ten grand to do a little job for him." Ginny shrugged. "It seemed easy enough. And ten grand is a lot of money."

For a tagging job? Sure is.

"He even gave me a hundred bucks to buy the paint with. He said it had to be red, and that he'd know if I didn't do it right."

"What did he look like?"

"White. Normal height. Muscular, maybe." Ginny shrugged. "I didn't really see him. He had some sort of cloak or shit on. Very gothic."

I raised my eyebrows, exchanging a look with Howell. "Did he have an English accent?"

Ginny frowned. "No. He didn't have any accent."

"Huh."

Howell took out his notepad. "No accent as in none whatsoever, or no accent as in he sounded like someone that belongs around here? With a *Ya'll might* and *Ope, 'scuse me, ma'am?*" He affected his speech with a deep southern drawl.

Ginny and I both turned to him.

"Excuse me?" I asked.

"He didn't sound like someone hit him over the head and knocked his brain loose, if that's what you mean," Ginny said angrily.

Howell raised his hands. "I'm sorry. But I'm not from around here, and you guys sound pretty odd sometimes."

Ginny crossed her arms and glared at Howell. "He sounded completely normal. No accent, not even a southern one."

I also crossed my arms. "Not everyone here has that strong of a southern accent, you know."

Howell sighed and dropped his notepad on the table. "I can tell I've struck a nerve, so I'm going to go get us some sodas."

Ginny and I both watched him leave.

"So, what happens now?" she asked.

"Now we're going to try to find this guy."

"And what happens to me?"

I thought for a second. "That really depends on Detective Howell, not me."

There was a quiet moment before the girl asked another question. "What's the symbol mean, then?"

I shook my head. "No idea."

Ginny hesitated, drumming her fingertips on the table. It was a cheap black folding table and it made a hollow note with each tap of her fingers. "Were you being serious about getting stripped and censored?"

I raised an eyebrow. "Yeah, I was." I leaned forward far enough to rest my forearms on the table. "So stop doing dumb shit. Especially with your magic."

She nodded. "I didn't realize that was something that could happen."

I drummed my own fingers on the tabletop. Howell was taking his sweet time at the vending machines. I took Howell's notepad and quickly wrote my number across the top page. "This is my cell number. I don't always answer, but you can leave a message for me."

Ginny made a face.

I rolled my eyes. "You can text me, too. Geez." I tore the paper off and handed it to her. "Call, or text me, if you ever have a question about magic or what you can and can't do. Or if you see that guy again. Got it?"

She took the paper with a nod and slipped it into the pocket of her hoodie.

My communicator chirped by my ear and I jumped in surprise.

"Ava?"

I'd completely forgotten I had it in. I turned the sudden movement into a stretch, but I don't think Ginny even noticed. "Alright, hang out here for a second. I'm going to go find out where our promised sodas went off to."

I stood and exited the interrogation room. The hallway outside was empty, so I parked my ass against the wall opposite the door I'd just come through. "Benji? What the hell took so long?" I whispered.

"I had to wait until Ross left. He's been watching me like a hawk all morning."

"Alright, give me what you've got."

"The autopsy on Feldman showed he died from multiple severed vertebrae. I could have told you that this morning."

"His neck was twisted like a chicken's," I said. "I know that much. And about the mark on the back of his right hand."

"There were also narcotics in his bloodstream. Lots of them."

"Anything else?"

"Yeah, there's another body," Benji said.

Howell turned the corner. He spotted me right away and quickened his pace. "Maxwell, they found the bouncer."

"Dead?" I asked.

Benji went silent on my comm.

Howell nodded. "Turned up in a dumpster behind the club. They saw him go on a smoke break shortly before Feldman's death, then he was seen again on camera again a few minutes later running like a bat outta hell."

"I've got the autopsy report right here, Ava," Benji said quietly. "Same cause of death as Feldman. Time of death is pretty much the same, too."

To Howell I said, "Let me guess, he died of a broken neck?"

Howell raised an eyebrow. "Two for two." He held a manila envelope up. "Care to guess what they found in his breast pocket?"

"Uhhh ..." I could hear the soft sounds of papers shuffling from Benji.

"A red felt pen," I answered, remembering the bouncer and his pocket protector. "Like the kind used to mark Feldman's hand."

"And a color photo of Feldman with that same symbol drawn underneath. In red ink."

"So, someone got to the bouncer and made the same deal to him as they did to Ginny? Gave him a photo of Feldman and a symbol to mark on his hand. Promise him something he can't refuse, like the ten grand he offered Ginny."

"Only instead of paying up, the bouncer gets killed too."

"He's cleaning up his mess as he makes it." I opened the door to the interrogation room with a bang, startling a shriek from Ginny.

I didn't even take the time to apologize to her for frightening her. "Do you still have the note that man gave you? The one with the symbol and the address you were supposed to tag?"

Ginny nodded. "It's in my bag."

I entered the room and made for the bag, which sat on the edge of the table closest to the door.

Howell followed right behind me. "What are you thinking, Maxwell?"

"I'm thinking that man had no intention of paying Ginny for her tagging job." I opened the backpack and dug through the contents. "And if the symbol he gave her is written in red ink, I think he fully intended for her to end up just as dead as Feldman and that bouncer." I turned the backpack over and shook it, sending cans of red spray paint rolling to the floor.

A small book fell to the table with a thump, and Ginny cried out. "Watch it, I'm reading that!"

A piece of paper was sticking out from between the pages like a bookmark. I pointed at it. "Is that it?"

"Yeah. I'm using it to mark my place."

"You're using a letter someone gave you to help you commit a crime as a bookmark?" I opened the book and glanced at the page number. "Get a real bookmark. Page 182." I tossed the book in her direction, letting it slap against the table again. The cover said something about fungi.

The paper was folded in half, and Howell came to stand beside me as I unfolded it. The paper was nothing special. Regular college lined loose-leaf paper. Written about halfway down was an address, likely Tooms's. Beneath that, in heavy red ink, was the symbol again.

"You seeing this?"

"I see it," both Benji and Howell said.

I crumpled the paper up into a tight ball. Howell protested immediately, but I pushed him away and channeled arcane energy into the palm that held the crumpled note. With a little more effort than I cared to admit, the paper burst into flames in my hand.

"What the hell, Maxwell?" Howell shouted. He slapped the burning paper from my hands and stomped on it, trying to put the fire out.

"Let it burn up, Howell." I put more energy into the fire, making sure it remained confined to the paper and didn't spread to Howell or his clothing. "That symbol is dangerous."

Howell looked at me, confused and panting slightly.

"Everyone that has been given that symbol or had it marked on them is dead." I pointed at Ginny. "Except for her, and except for—"

"Tooms," Howell finished.

"Get a car down there to check on him." I turned to the girl. "Ginny."

She jumped at the sound of her name. She'd been watching the fire burn, her face pale.

"You're going to have to stay here for a few hours. For your own protection. Howell will make sure you're comfortable."

The flame went out with a sudden poof, and I took a steadying breath. It shouldn't have been so hard to do that little trick. But I hadn't slept since the night before last, and I hadn't had a real meal in nearly as long. That was what I got for working through lunch. And dinner ... and breakfast.

Howell took Ginny by the shoulders, gathered up her empty backpack and led her out of the room.

When the door shut behind them, Benji spoke up again from my communicator. "What do you need from me?"

I thought for a moment. Howell had come running to me as soon as he had learned about the bouncer's death. He hadn't thought for a moment about keeping me in the dark.

"Just keep Ross from finding out I'm still working this case."

"I'll do what I can. Jackson out."

I pulled out my cell phone and searched the contacts for Frankie's awful contact name. It rang three times before he answered.

"Hello?"

"Frankie, I need a hand." My voice echoed, and I realized he had me on speaker.

"And I need a month or so without your number showing up on my phone."

I ignored the shit talk and dove on ahead. "What's your favorite occult store, preferably here in Norman, and are they open right now?"

"My favorite what now?"

"Occult store. I know you and Dorian frequent them, even though you're a scientist and you're supposed to be levelheaded and you're not supposed to believe in that nonsense."

"Excuse me?" Frankie asked in a whiny falsetto. "I don't know what you're talking about, ho."

"Cut the shit for a moment, Frankie. A girl's life may be in danger."

"The Quill and Kettle. Or maybe the Quill and Cauldron. We just call it the Quill," an effeminate voice answered. "It's down on Campus Corner. Tiny store across from the copy shop. She closes at sundown every day."

"Thank you, Dorian," I said with a grateful sigh. "Frankie, you should learn from Dorian. He's nice. He's helpful. And he's not a massive dick about it."

"He might not *be* one," Frankie said, "but he sure does have—"

I hung up and headed for the Blackbird.

Howell caught up with me in the parking lot. "I've got a patrol car on the way to check on Tooms. Where are you going?"

"I'm going to find out what that symbol means. Just keep Ginny safe." I unlocked the tail box and removed my helmet.

"Be careful, Ava. You know where I'll be if you need to get in touch."

He used my first name. It sounded kind of weird.

"Sure thing … Phil," I said, remembering what Ross had called him that morning.

Howell made a face. "Not Phil. Only Ellis calls me Phil."

"You prefer Howell?"

"I prefer Phillip."

"Nerd." I slipped the helmet over my head and started the Blackbird.

Howell stepped back and I rode off for the university campus.

CHAPTER

EIGHT

T raffic was getting rough. It was almost noon, and the streets were filled with people getting out for lunch. It only got worse as I neared campus. I had to contend with people coming to campus for the restaurants as well as students driving in for afternoon classes. It took nearly half an hour to make the relatively short drive from the center of town to the southern end where the campus sat.

There were only a few areas around the university campus with motorcycle parking and not many people used those spots, which usually guaranteed I could find parking, but also meant I had to walk a few blocks to get to where I needed to be. Normally it was a mild inconvenience, but the extra few minutes it took for me to walk a block or two weren't usually the potential difference between life and death.

If that mysterious symbol really was being used to mark people for death, then there wasn't any time at all to waste. And if Mr. Hook or his non-accented accomplice were the ones determining who got marked ...

My head hurt just trying to piece it all together coherently.

Ginny's life was in danger because she made a deal with a stranger who promised her ten thousand dollars.

The sheer stupidity of it made my head ache more.

So I parked on the sidewalk, right in front of the store Dorian had told me about.

The Quill was indeed a tiny store, tucked between a Chinese restaurant and an empty storefront with a For Lease sticker in the window. A large wooden sign hung over the door. Most other shops in the city had departed from similar signage in favor of large and easily replaceable plastic letters with lights wired in, or the much simpler vinyl stick-on letters tacked to doors with glass inlays.

I glanced up briefly at the sign as I parked the Blackbird. It featured a stylized quill and a pot of some sort. The letters were also heavily stylized and difficult to read from my angle. It could have said *Cauldron* or *Kettle*. I really couldn't tell either way.

The door, *sans* glass insert and vinyl lettering, was painted a cheery turquoise and covered in runes and symbols in white chalk. I opened the door and entered, not entirely sure whether to expect a dark and musty store with creepy-looking ingredients on shelves or a brightly lit hippie paradise of bundled sage and marijuana buds.

It was neither.

Tiny sage bundles were arranged in a low basket right by the front door. A small sign affixed to the basket read "Free Smudge Stick with Every Visit!" in neat cursive. Soft yellow light bathed every surface and created a relaxing and welcoming ambience. And it smelled nice. Like vanilla, but not the heavy kind used in perfumes. It smelled like real vanilla.

Low tables were covered in typical spiritual wellness merchandise in four neat rows and tall glass-fronted cabinets stood on each of the long side walls. There were baskets of worry stones and posters of constellation charts and a soy candle in the shape of a pair of breasts. A rack contained incense sticks and cones arranged by scent. Each scent had a little tag listing the best intentions for its use. A bulk pack of one hundred mix-and-match sticks sold for fifteen bucks.

Hidden speakers played a soundtrack of ocean waves with some sort of soft flute music. And there were a lot of books. Books for sale, books on display, books stacked artfully on rattan stools. Just a bunch of books. Everywhere. I could see why Frankie and Dorian enjoyed the atmosphere of the place, even if I couldn't quite understand what they ever bought here. Maybe the incense.

Directly opposite the door, on the far wall, was a counter with the only modern contraptions in the whole room—an open silver laptop and a white payment system. The kind with a little pad that you can rotate around to get signatures and such.

There was no one in sight.

"Hello?" I called, approaching the counter.

"Just a second!"

It was a woman's voice, and it came from behind a small door set into the same wall the counter was on.

I waited, listening to the faint sounds of scuffling and what might have been cardboard boxes scraping against the floor.

There was a pause and a soft curse.

"Need a hand back there?" I asked.

"Can you lift about fifty pounds?"

I thought for a second. "Yeah, I think so."

"Then yeah, I could use a hand."

I opened the door. I'm not really considered tall for a

woman, but I instinctively stooped slightly to go through the doorway.

Beyond the door was a storage room of sorts. Two ceiling-height metal racks were stacked with boxes and crates, and a ladder roughly four feet tall was opened in front of an open spot near the top of one rack.

A woman stood by the ladder with a box at her feet. Her face was flushed. "I hate doing inventory. I can never handle the heavy boxes well." She flashed a cute and apologetic smile and brushed a frazzled lock of ginger curls from her face.

I shrugged. "I'm sure the two of us can get it up there."

I climbed the ladder, pressing my hips and thighs against the narrow frame, and reached for the box. The woman passed it up to me, and I hefted it with one hand while steadying myself with the other. It was definitely not fifty pounds. More like thirty. But it was still awkward to handle on the ladder.

"Here, I've got you."

I felt a pair of hands on the backs of my thighs, pushing me lightly into the ladder and helping me keep my balance.

Don't let the Bi out, nope, nope, nope, I thought furiously as I lifted the box up to shoulder height and shoved it into place.

"Sorry," the woman said. "I normally wine and dine an attractive woman before bringing her to the shop to do hard labor with me."

I smiled down at her. "Sometimes it's nice to mix things up a bit."

Aaand, there goes the Bi in me. Out.

I descended the ladder and turned to shake the woman's hand. "I'm Ava."

"Freya."

I raised an eyebrow. "Freya, as in ..."

She nodded. "As in Norse mythology, yes. And yes, it is my real name."

"I like it. I bet it suits you well."

We shook.

"What brings you in, Ava? Something I can help you with, I hope."

And just like that, I pushed aside the not-insignificant part of me that was calculating the length of time since I had last been on a date and trying to decide if Freya was into women or was just being polite and returned to the business at hand.

"I hope so, too. I'm a detective—"

"With the APD, I assume?"

"Yeah," I said, surprised. "How did you know?"

Freya opened the door back to the shop and motioned me through. "You've got a strong aura. Not something you'd normally see on the mundane police force."

I was flattered. I'd never thought of my own aura as particularly strong.

"Well, I've got a strange symbol that keeps coming up in the case I'm working. Would you mind taking a look and seeing what you think about it?"

Freya frowned. "You don't have a symbolist on staff?"

I was sure we did, but getting our own symbolist involved would require going to Ross and giving him hard evidence that I had been going behind his back and working on the Dust case.

"Time is of the essence, and getting our symbolist to look into this would take way too long."

Freya shrugged a shoulder. "Alright, I can take a look. Runes and symbols aren't my strong suit, but I do find them interesting. I can maybe help."

I took the drawing Howell had done for me that

morning and set it on the counter. "It looks like this, but the one we keep seeing is red."

"Red?" Freya asked.

"Yeah." I remembered Ginny describing the mystery man's insistence that she draw the symbol properly. "It seems really important that it be red."

Freya nodded. "Colors in symbols are important. They help to convey intention. I'm surprised you didn't know already."

Ouch.

"So, what does red mean?"

Freya sighed. "It depends on the symbol. Passion, typically. But the kind of passion is determined by the symbol. A red heart, as a simple example, would not mean the same as a red knife."

"Alright. And this symbol?" I tapped the paper.

Freya chewed at a fingernail. "It looks vaguely familiar. But it's not one I recognize offhand. Give me a second." She went around to the other side of the counter and knelt to rummage through yet another stack of books arranged on a shelf below the laptop. "I keep a bunch of reference books back here for occasions just like this, but it might take a few minutes for me to find what I'm looking for."

She lifted a large book, easily twelve by twelve inches and about four inches thick, and dropped it onto the counter with a slam. "You're free to have a look around."

I wandered the small store while Freya turned pages and mumbled to herself. The store was quite comfortable. There was even a plush reading nook with an oil diffuser. The vanilla scent seemed strongest in that direction. The whole place was meant to be relaxing and inviting, but I still felt irritated at being forced to wait for answers.

I wasn't ever good at sitting around patiently.

"How long have you been here, Freya?"

"Mm, not long. Five years? But my family has been in the occult business for generations."

"And it's just you running this place?"

Freya nodded, not looking up from her reference book. "It's easier to keep overheads low when you don't have employees. And I'm only open from sunup to sundown ten months out of the year."

I raised an eyebrow. "And the other two months?"

She smiled. "Most of my clients are curious college students. I pack up when they leave town. I have a few dedicated clients, but they know my schedule and know to stock up their goods before the shop is closed for summer."

I examined a small book with a detailed illustration of a couple mid-coitus on the cover. "Must be nice to take the summer off, though."

"It is. I go to Belize for two weeks and then spend the rest of the time restocking some of the harder-to-find ingredients for the store."

I spotted a display case inside one of the glass-fronted cabinets. There was a lock on it, and inside were several small burlap bags with handwritten tags affixed to them. One read "Refined Egyptian Blue Lotus, $75/g. Controlled substance, ID and proper paperwork req. for sale."

"I think I understand the kind of restocking you mean." I glanced up in her direction. "I'm assuming you have the proper permits to sell refined substances?"

"Of course, Detective." Freya gave me a coy look.

I resumed my exploring.

"You're pacing," Freya said.

"I'm shopping." I picked up the nearest item and held it up for her. It happened to be the boob candle. "How much for this?"

"Twenty-five plus tax." She didn't even look up. Freya was about a third of the way through the hefty book.

"For a pair of wax breasts?" I asked in disbelief.

"It's used for fertility and certain intimacy rituals." She looked up as she turned another page. "And it's a miniaturized version of a bust I did of my own breasts."

"Well, now I've got to have it."

Freya smirked. "It's yours. One time deal. Only for that item, and only because you're cute as hell."

Still got it.

I put the candle back and continued my nervous walk around the store. I thought of calling the Norman Police Department to get in touch with Howell, but I hadn't been gone for very long and there was no news yet to share. So instead I sniffed at incense sticks. Most of them smelled like typical incense scents you could buy from any hippie store or pot shop. I expected the notes underneath to be very generic or a bit silly, like *Use for cleansing negative energy* or *Best for opening the crown chakra*. And there were a few like that. In fact each of the seven chakras had its own incense scent. But there was also one labeled *Great for getting rid of your ex's scent from your home*. It smelled like something green and earthy. There was also a small sign that stated more scents were available upon request. I suspected the more arcane-oriented scents were held back from mundane customers.

"Ava, I think I found it."

I hurried back over to the counter, going around to stand behind it.

Freya pointed to a symbol drawn in thick black lines. "It's not identical, but it has some similarities."

She was right. Some lines were missing here and there, but the overall shape was the same.

"What is it used for?" I scanned the text surrounding the image. I couldn't understand it. "Is this ... Latin?"

Freya scoffed, turning back a page to the section header. "You don't know Latin? What kind of arcanist are you?"

"The kind that can't read Latin," I retorted. "What does it say?"

She frowned. "Nothing good, I'm afraid. Symbols like that are used for summoning demons."

I was speechless for a second. "Demon summoning is illegal."

Freya shrugged. "Lots of things are illegal. Doesn't mean they don't still happen."

I considered the information for a moment. "How would that work?"

"Well ..." Freya looked uncomfortable. "According to this, you would mark the symbol on the focus of the demon's attention." She looked at me. "Using the proper color for the intention, of course."

"Red, in this case," I added.

"And then the same symbol is used during the summoning." She turned the page again. "Altering the structure of the symbol will release the demon from the summoning and allow it to run free for as long as the summoning lasts. Simply marking through it with black ink will negate the energy tied to it."

"And then the demon will visit each symbol and perform the intended function."

Freya nodded.

"And red for a demon symbol could be used for murderous intent?"

Freya made a face. "It is a very fitting color."

Shit.

"How long does a summoning last?"

"Twenty-four hours."

Double shit.

"Is there a way to tell where the symbol may have been left?"

Freya raised an eyebrow. "Before the demon finds it? Not really. After the demon finds it ..."

"After the demon finds it, you've got a dead body."

Her face went a little pale.

"Is there a way to find out where the summoning took place?"

"Maybe." Freya chewed on her fingernail again. "If the summoning is still active, then it would be giving off a lot of energy. You would need something vital to the summoning or the summoner to locate it, though."

Like a vial of Dust, perhaps?

Freya shrugged and added. "Or you could get the demon to lead you to it, but you'd have to find a way to capture it. And that's not easy."

That piqued my interest. "But not impossible, right?"

Freya stared at me for a moment like I was insane. And perhaps I was.

When I finally left the Quill, the first thing I heard was my cell phone ringing. I thought for a moment I had left it in my bike again, but it was in my pants pocket.

The number had an old exchange code I recognized as the one all City of Norman offices used. I answered it.

"Howell?"

"Yeah, it's me." Howell's breath was heavy, like he'd been running. "Just got a call from the cruiser sitting by Tooms's place. They heard shouts and screams, so they stormed in."

"Fuck, please don't tell me."

"Tooms is dead, Maxwell. No one saw anyone enter or leave the house." I heard a car door slam. "I'm heading there now to check it out."

"I'm on my way."

NINE

I got to Tooms's neighborhood in time to see his body being wheeled out on a stretcher. His neighbors stood on porches and in their tiny yards to whisper and stare as he was loaded into an ambulance. The lights on the ambulance weren't even flashing. Tooms would not be going to the hospital. He was already in a black body bag, and he would soon be in the medical examiner's office for an autopsy.

I scanned the faces but only recognized a few of the officers and one of the paramedics. None of them were APD, though the paramedic had a fair bit of arcane energy in his aura, if I remembered correctly. His name was Rogers or something similar.

I waved down an officer I recognized from the crime scene this morning. He was on his way out to a forensics van with a black toolbox that was likely full of collected evidence.

"Where's Howell?"

The officer stopped long enough to give me a quick glance before gesturing off to the back of the house and hurrying on his way.

I thought about telling him that they were wasting their time collecting evidence. That the killer didn't leave anything behind, or rather that he *couldn't* leave anything behind, but I didn't really have the time to argue with someone about demons. Howell would understand, hopefully.

There were two or three officers on crowd control. Not that there was really much of a crowd to control. They gave me no trouble as I hurried past them. The two trash cans had been picked up by the city waste management since Howell and I had left that morning. The bins sat slightly askew and with both their lids open. I stepped on a bit of missed debris and looked down to see it was a crushed white and red cigarette pack.

Dammit, Tooms.

I didn't like the guy, not in the least. But I had known him. More than I had known Feldman, at any rate. And it felt strange to be at the crime scene for the murder of someone I knew.

I turned the corner to the back of the house, my eyes still on the cigarette pack I had stepped on. "Howell, I—"

"Maxwell," a deep voice said. "I should have known you would get yourself involved, despite the suspension."

I came to a surprised stop. "Captain Ross."

Ross stood with Howell in front of the symbol still painted on the side of Toom's house. There were signs of some halfhearted attempts to clean it, but the symbol was only smudged, not erased.

I looked from Ross to Howell and back again. "What are you doing here?"

Ross's eyebrows raised. "My job, Detective. Something I should have done from the start of this Dust mess, since you don't seem to care enough about your work to do it properly."

"Ellis has assigned himself to this case as the APD liaison," Howell added. He looked flustered, perhaps even angry. "From this point on, he and I will be partnering on this Dust investigation and the associated murders."

"Oh, good." I tried to hide my annoyance behind an air of professionalism. "I was worried you still hadn't received any assistance from APD, so I came to offer my help."

"Cut the crap, Maxwell," Ross said. "I know you and Phil have been working on this case together. You went to the first crime scene this morning, and then the two of you were here only hours ago to interview Mr. Tooms about Feldman's death."

And how the hell does he know that?

"Evidently, Ellis has been kept apprised of our progress so far." There was a dull redness to Howell's face, as if he and Ross had been arguing heatedly, and his forehead wrinkled into a deep frown.

I sighed. *Dammit, Benji. I thought we were going to keep this from Ross. And instead you've been feeding everything from my comm line right to him.*

"What did you find out about the symbol, Maxwell?" Ross asked.

Had Benji missed the conversation at the Quill?

For the first time in my still fairly short career as an APD officer, I told a direct and bold-faced lie to my commanding officer.

"Nothing yet." I shrugged. "It doesn't match anything I've seen before. I was going to call in a favor and have a friend look into it—"

"No," Ross shook his head. "No more friends, Maxwell. You seem to keep forgetting that we're public servants, not private investigators. We're bound by different rules."

Howell stared at me. I ignored him in favor of Ross, who

was much larger and more intimidating. And who, at the moment, I didn't trust at all.

"Go home, Maxwell. Phil and I will take over from here." Ross stepped closer, practically looming over me. "And if I see you again today, you will be fired. Do you understand?"

I nodded. "Sure."

Ross motioned back towards the street. "Do you need an escort off of the scene, Miss Maxwell?"

"Nope, I think I can find my way." I turned on my heel and walked off. I waited until I'd turned the corner and was back on the gravel and asphalt road before pulling the silver studs out of my ears and pocketing them.

The onlookers were mostly gone, as was the ambulance. The walk back to my Blackbird was uneventful, giving me a few moments to figure out the hazy beginnings of a plan. I pulled up my recent calls on my cell phone and redialed one.

"City of Norman Police Department," a harried male's voice said. "You know the extension you want?"

"No, actually. But the name is Howell."

"Detective Howell is in the field right now, I believe. Would you like me to forward you to his cell?"

"No, I can just leave a message on his desk line."

"Directing you now."

I left a very short message, less than five seconds, and hung up.

By my estimation, Ross would keep Howell occupied on the scene for at least another two hours. There would be no leaving until every scrap of evidence had been collected and they had thoroughly walked the scene. Howell and I both knew how Tooms died. I didn't need to see the body to guess that he'd had his neck snapped.

But Ross was a man that did everything exactly to the

letter, even if it meant he was losing ground on a case while doing so.

And I hoped that the first thing Howell would do when finally free to return to his office would be to call in and check his voicemail. It's not what I would personally do, but I'm not as put together and organized as Howell.

And two hours would give me plenty of time to do my own running around.

My first stop was at a hardware store. I chose the one that happened to have the easiest drive over to my favorite fried-chicken-tender spot. There was technically one closer to Tooms's place, but I had time. And, as I still had not eaten anything substantial since Frankie's cold ramen, I was going to need something hot and greasy and covered in proprietary sauce fairly soon or I would start losing it.

The store was surprisingly busy for a weekday afternoon. I thought I knew the layout of the store well enough to find everything I needed, but I had to stop and ask an employee for directions. His name was Tim. Tim was very helpful and did not at all look suspicious of the items on my list. Maybe they saw all kinds of questionable purchases at big hardware stores.

In the end, I deliberated on the items in my cart for several minutes and walked out with only two things. Well, two of one thing and one of a second thing, so I guess three things altogether.

It all fit nicely in the tail box of the Blackbird, along with the tiny bag from the Quill that had already been riding around with me. From there, it was a quick ride over to pick up some chicken tenders. I got the largest meal they offered, then added extra tenders, extra sauce, and extra fries. I did skip the drink, though.

I was really damn hungry.

And I don't think well when I'm hungry.

It was a couple of hours after lunch, in that quiet dead time in the early afternoon that a lot of fast-food places experience, and during which I seemed to always end up ordering. It took some time, but my obnoxiously large order came. I shoveled a few fresh fries into my mouth before tucking the entire fast-food bag into the tail box. The smell would weep into the lining, but it wasn't the first time I'd put fast food back there and likely wouldn't be the last.

I checked my cell before riding for home. No message from Howell. I wasn't expecting one, but it would have been a mild comfort. I reckoned just under an hour before Howell might be free of Ross's annoying oversight. Hopefully I would have just enough time to get home, get my supplies unloaded and ready to go, and then shovel copious amounts of fried foods into my face hole before Howell got my message and we met up to begin our proper detective work again. And I still had to review the test reports Frankie had left in my home office.

The weather was nice, with some big puffy clouds and a light cooling breeze to contend with the spring sun. And to think we'd just had a horrid snowstorm only a few weeks before. But that was Oklahoma.

The streets were fairly empty, a far cry from the busy lunch hour traffic I had fought through earlier, and I spent the short ride racking my brain for any idea of who else might be targeted.

I had been upset about my small list of suspects when it came to trying to stop Dust from spreading through the streets of the Oklahoma metro. But now that it came to identifying potential victims, I was grateful. I didn't want any more deaths on my conscience.

I parked in the driveway, careful to make my Blackbird easy to spot, and entered through the garage with my various purchases in my arms. Half of the garage was a mess of exercise equipment and storage boxes full of forgotten hobbies. The other half housed the entrance to the in-ground tornado shelter no Oklahoma home is complete without, and a few oil and grease spots from various afternoons spent working on the motorcycle. I snacked on another fry or two and made a mental note to change the garage's keypad code as the mechanical lift whirred behind me.

I struggled to the kitchen and dropped my various bags on the counter. There was an empty summer sausage wrapper sitting right in the center, with a pastel blue sticky note that read "I left a mess, watchu gonna do about it?" in heavy lettering.

"Dammit, Frankie."

I dumped my hardware store purchases and my bag from the Quill on the counter and popped open the styrofoam food container. The food was still hot, and moisture had accumulated along the top of the lid. The smell of fried chicken tenders instantly filled the kitchen, and my stomach rumbled loudly. I slipped off my tennis shoes and snagged a tender to munch on while I padded across the carpeted living room to the office.

Frankie's report likely wouldn't tell me anything I could coherently understand and didn't already know, but he had done me a huge solid. I wasn't going to just ignore it.

I stopped in the doorway to the office.

The drawers to my cheap desk had been pulled open, and papers were scattered across the floor. My laptop, which I had left open and waiting for me, had been smashed and lay on its side beside the trashcan, which had been emptied and tossed across the room. And there was a familiar metallic tang of ozone in the air.

"What the fuck?" I mumbled around a mouthful of food.

I set the half-eaten strip of chicken on the desk and shuffled through the few pages that remained on the desk. They were case notes. Not from the Pixie Dust case, but from an older one that had been passed off to Norman PD a month ago, redacted copies I had kept on hand in case I was called in for further help.

I picked up another handful of papers.

More case notes. Some handwritten sticky notes that no longer had a page to stick to. And a couple of black and white photos from a surveillance I worked down in Lawton the year before.

Not a single page was from the Dust case. And Frankie's reports were nowhere to be seen.

"Shit."

I dropped the papers and ran for the kitchen. My phone was still on the counter, I remembered, and I raced for it. Forget subtleties and working behind Ross's back. I needed to get in touch with Howell now. My phone was right where I had left it—right next to the two cans of black spray paint I'd bought half an hour before. I grabbed it and dialed frantically, working from memory.

A terrifying thought hit me, and I started for the front door. If someone had taken the time to break into my home and steal every last slip of paper I had on the Dust case, then there was a good chance they might have left a certain mark on my home.

I didn't have to go very far to find it.

It was painted in thick brushstrokes on my front door.

The *inside* of my front door, where I wouldn't have immediately seen it when pulling into the driveway.

I hesitated, cell phone in hand, staring at the dull and dry symbol.

"Shit," I said again.

And then I was struck hard from behind.

TEN

Thanks to the shielding spell in my bracer, the hit didn't send me flying through the house to hit the front door with a sickening crunch. Instead, I just hit the front door with a loud bang and a cry of pain. The shielding spell was designed to reflect impacts and rebound them, not to entirely absorb them. So, instead of letting me slump gracefully to the floor, the impact of my body hitting the door was reflected. I immediately bounced back several feet and landed painfully on my back.

I stared up at the ceiling, trying to catch my breath and making a mental note to vacuum the cobwebs hanging in the corners. "Shit," I muttered weakly, repeating the mantra for the third time.

The scent of rotting meat filled my nose, and a very large, very clawed hand reached down to grab my entire freaking face. I'll admit that I panicked and yelled incoherently. I also summoned what energy I could in the milliseconds I had before my head could be ripped from my shoulders and sent it out in a blast of unfocused terror.

The hand disappeared. So did the fetid stink of rot and whatever unspeakable monstrosity was connected to the two. I heard something heavy collide with several metallic objects in a series of crashes and heavy thumps.

I quickly rolled over to my front and scrambled to my feet.

A huge and indistinct mass of black was squirming on the floor of my formal dining-room-turned-workout room, partially blocking my path. Whatever it was, it was buried in dumbbells. My energy blast had evidently sent it colliding into one of my weight racks, hence the metal clanging I had heard.

I focused on the *thing* on my floor and blinked. I blinked again, and then a few more times just for good measure.

Remember what I said about auras? That everything has an aura except demons, and one does not fuck with demons?

The thing on my floor had no aura. In fact, not only did it not have an aura, it had an insane-looking kind of energy vacuum where an aura should have been. I had never seen anything like it, and it was honestly painful to stare at for too long. The halo around the demon that had just tried to skin my face was indistinct and impossible to look directly at without becoming blurry.

I broke the aura check and made for the kitchen, jumping over the prone demon.

I didn't quite clear the demon, instead landing painfully on one knee and both forearms. The impact with the door must have burned out the energy stored in my bracer, because I took the full brunt of the landing.

There was a very sickening *pop* from my left shoulder, and I let out a pained wail.

I was going to feel like hell if I survived the next few minutes.

Once again, I scrambled to my feet. I heard the creature behind me doing the same. One of us was cursing horribly.

The other was making inhuman and unearthly sounds of fury.

I reached for the bag from the Quill. I barely got my hand around the paper handles when a hand clasped around my left ankle and tore me down to the floor. Everything on the counter was swept to the floor with me. The black spray paint. The lantern I'd bought for nighttime symbol searching. And my fucking chicken. It hit the floor with a smack, and my little cup of delicious sauce split open and rolled across the floor.

I screamed. It was a deep, guttural, hungry scream. The demon was pulling me back towards the front door, and I turned onto my back and faced it.

It looked like something between a huge, hellish dog and a boar. The snout was canine, with two long tusks emerging from either side. It was solid black, hairless, and naked. It stood on four muscular legs, each one ending in a very human hand. One such hand held me painfully by the leg. And the eyes were a deep crimson. There was no intelligence to them that I could see. Only anger and an urge to kill.

I'm sure my eyes held something very similar.

I swung the paper bag, hitting the demon square on the nose. "You ugly little bitch!" I screamed. I hit him again. "You ruined my fucking dinner."

The strikes didn't faze the beast in the slightest. His head didn't even jerk with each blow.

I changed tactics.

I drew in a deep breath, pulling more arcane energy through my body to focus on my hands. It was uncomfortable, like needles poking into your skin, or the sensation you get when a limb falls asleep and then starts to get the blood circulating again.

Arcane energy was historically channeled through the use of wands, but wands grew out of fashion during the witch hunts of the sixteenth and seventeenth centuries. Some older arcanists used staffs, which were easier to explain away as stylized walking sticks, but most now used nothing at all. The sensation of tapping into your arcane essence and burning it away for a bit of glamor magic or conjuration took some getting used to, but it was usually painless.

It was only the big magic, the kind you might use to fend off a demon intent on snapping your neck like a twig, that still hurt like hell.

I bought a few seconds by kicking the big ugly beast in the nose. I was only wearing socks—I'd taken off my shoes shortly after coming into the house—and I knew my hits weren't going to do much damage. I had to bring my knee up clear to my chest to get enough clearance to hit him, and I only landed two blows before he had pulled me close enough to pin me down with a second hand. His claws pinched painfully at my sides, but they did not cut me. The demon only applied enough pressure to keep me down and not enough to really crush me.

He's playing with me.

I ground my teeth. I could smell the charge of arcane energy in the air. It was remarkably similar to ozone.

That disgusting rotting meat stench hit me, and it grew stronger as the beast leaned over my face. His mouth opened, and a thick black tongue lolled out. Where saliva might have dripped from a dog's mouth, steam billowed from the demon's mouth instead.

And then it spoke. "Any last words, Miss Maxwell?"

The damned thing had a polite English accent.

I blinked. "Yeah, actually," I said slowly. I dropped the paper bag I'd been holding and brought my hands up in surrender. My left arm mostly just flopped painfully, and I realized I'd dislocated the shoulder in my fall.

The demon's mouth twisted into an ugly grin. "Yes?"

"Fuck. Off."

I blasted the hairless demon boar thing right in its hideous face with nearly every drop of arcane energy I had in me.

The demon let out a yelp of pain and smashed into something that splintered. I was scrambling to my feet and didn't bother to see where the beastly thing had landed. I shook the paper bag from the Quill out onto the floor and bent to hastily pick up the talisman Freya had lent me. I had to keep my left arm tucked into my middle to avoid crying out in pain.

The talisman was shaped like a simple block of wood and was the perfect size for my fingers to wrap nicely around it. In the center was a large gemstone. It looked like a huge diamond, but Freya had insisted it was only a cut chunk of clear quartz. Beneath the stone was a carved depiction of a keyhole.

I straightened and widened my stance, hoping like hell what I was about to do was going to actually work. Some twenty feet away, right in the entryway to my house, the demon was standing unsteadily on all fours.

It gave a mighty shake of its weird head before locking gazes with me and staring me down. It hunched slightly, muscles tensing.

I bent my knees and took on a one-armed grappling stance, the talisman tight in my hand. My ankle flared painfully with even that small movement, but I wasn't ready to fall over and die just yet.

I rolled my only functioning shoulder. "Bring it, bitch."

The demon charged, howling as it went.

I made my own battle cry, though I think mine was a string of angry curses.

Just before we connected, I spun away, pressing the talisman against the demon's hindquarters as I did. Freya had said just a touch of the gemstone against the weakened demon would be enough to seal it away, and I had made definite contact with the demon's ugly rump.

I had a brief moment of satisfaction when I mentally tallied my long list of successful battles against demons. Ava, one. Demons, zero.

And then the fucking thing pounced. Like a cat attacking a toy mouse.

Except I was the toy mouse.

Perhaps the demon had anticipated my move, or perhaps it was just much more agile than I had originally thought. But two huge hands came down on me and knocked me against the back of my couch.

I managed to hold on to the talisman by virtue of sheer luck, and my head snapped back painfully. The couch slid several inches, and I quickly lost my support and went crashing to the floor, demon on top of me. I screamed profanities as my injured shoulder was jostled and jerked far too much.

I squirmed, lifting the talisman high enough to smack it against the side of the demon's face. It did nothing. "Why won't you just die?"

The demon laughed, its tongue rolling out of its mouth again. Hot, disgusting breath was blasted into my face, and I would have gagged if I wasn't so focused on grappling with the beast before it could snap my neck. I wrapped my legs around the thing's hips, trying to use my lower body strength to pull it off my chest and shoulders while simultaneously prying long claws from my hair. The demon didn't budge.

Three loud gunshots pierced the air in quick succession. I saw the bullets strike the demon in the shoulder, several inches from my face, with soft impact sounds and small bursts of steam.

"Maxwell?"

"Howell?" I couldn't turn to see him because the demon had my head pinned to the ground, but I recognized his voice.

Howell shot twice more, and the demon growled and released me.

"Shit," Howell said. "It won't go down."

The demon was rising to its hind legs, breaking my various holds on it with ease. It turned to face the front door, and I rolled onto my front to see Howell standing some five feet inside the house.

Howell still had his gun raised, but he looked uncertain. "Maxwell?"

"You can't shoot a fucking demon, Howell." There was a can of spray paint inches from Howell's foot, and I pointed at it. "Paint a line through the symbol on the door. Hurry!"

The demon was sizing Howell up, as if determining which of the two of us was the bigger threat at the moment. And all signs pointed to the big guy with the gun rather than the bruised and tired girl on the floor.

I staggered to my feet for what I really hoped would be the last time that evening and tackled the demon from behind. We both went down, and I gave a pained cry as my shoulder collided with something hard and bony. I once more grappled with the beast, pulling one of its strange limbs to its side and hooking my legs around its waist. The massive thing writhed and howled. A claw cut me across the forearm, and my skin itched and burned horribly where it had made contact. Bright red blood welled out of the wound.

I heard the spray can rattling. "Howell," I called.

"Just a minute."

More rattling. But no hissing sounds of spray painting. I chanced a look up to see Howell frantically shaking the can and staring at the half-opened front door. My door frame had been busted, either by Howell or the demon when I'd sent it flying.

The demon let out an almighty jerk, almost bucking me off, and snapped his huge teeth at me. Its tusks left rends in my carpet. I punched it in the face.

"Howell!"

"Just a minute, Maxwell." Howell finally uncapped the can and looked over the symbol on the door.

"For fuck's sake, Howell. You're not Banksy, just cross the damn symbol out!"

He did. One long swipe of black spread over the red symbol with a quick pass of the can in Howell's hand.

The demon let out a high-pitched, porcine squeal and thrashed in my grip. I held it as tightly as I could with my legs and pressed the talisman to its head. It gave another piercing shriek and then simply disappeared.

I fell to the ground face first, smacking my nose and forehead on the ground.

"Maxwell? You alright?"

Howell helped me roll onto my back, and I cradled my arm, now cut as well as popped out of the shoulder socket, to my chest. I lay that way for a moment, staring up at the ceiling of my house again. Howell sat on the floor beside my head, pressing one of my tea towels to my arm.

"Shit," I groaned. "What a damn day."

Howell helped me sit up. "I got your message about twenty minutes after you sent it. I've been watching this house from down the block. Who lives here, and how did you know the demon would show up?"

I gave him a tired glare. "I live here. And I didn't."

"Then why tell me to meet you here?"

I stood up, letting Howell help me further. "So we could go over the Dust case without Ross breathing down our necks." I leaned against the kitchen counter, staring at the blood-soaked towel my arm was wrapped in. "My nice tea towel ..." I stared at the chicken tenders spread on the floor and squashed into little messy piles and the trail of light red sauce across my kitchen tiles. "My dinner."

I honestly wanted to cry. Just a little. Out of anger. And hunger.

"Come on, let's get you cleaned up and get this called in. Where's the bathroom?"

I started numbly for the bathroom. "Call what in? You seriously want me to tell the Norman police I was attacked by a demon summoned to murder anyone related to the weird new street drug they probably have only just started hearing about?"

"We can tell them it was an intruder."

"What's the point? They won't find any intruder. And you fired a bunch of shots, but the only blood on the scene is mine." I winced as my ankle flared in pain again. "My neighbors know I'm with the police. I doubt any of them called anyone."

Howell paused. "I guess that's true."

I stopped and gave him another tired glare. "Did any of your shots miss?"

Howell shook his head.

"Well at least I don't have to worry about digging bullets out of the drywall."

ELEVEN

In the end, one neighbor did call the police. Or, to be more precise, she called the number I had given her for my partner, and Benjamin Jackson pulled up in my driveway, lights rolling, while Howell was fashioning a sling for my arm.

"Ava?"

I heard his boots clomping around the front of my house, and I looked under Howell's arm to catch sight of him standing in the center of what had been my open kitchen and living room area. "Over here, Benji."

Howell helped me stand, and I hobbled over to meet Benji. My ankle was swollen, and purple bruises had already formed in a thick ring around it where the demon had pulled me around. My forearm was also bandaged, and Howell had confirmed a dislocated shoulder before rudely popping it back into place for me.

"Geez, Ava. Shouldn't you be at the hospital? What happened?"

"She won't go to the hospital," Howell grumbled. "Trust me, I've tried."

Benji took another look around the room while Howell

sat on the arm of my couch. "Seriously, what the hell happened?"

"Demon attack," I answered.

"Shit, here?" Benji's hand immediately went to his gun, but I raised a hand to calm him.

"Relax, it's gone. Hopefully for good."

Benji did not relax. Instead he stared at me like I had grown a second head. "But why here?"

I bent to pick up a torn and smashed chicken tender and tossed it onto the kitchen island. "Good question. The only reasonable answer I can come up with is that we have a mole in the department."

Benji cursed again. Howell made no sign of surprise at all.

"Are you sure?" Benji asked.

"The symbol we keep finding at the crime scenes was painted on Maxwell's front door," Howell said. "On the inside of the door."

I nodded, glad he had caught on.

"Which means someone knew how to gain entrance to her home without raising suspicion."

"Who would know how to do that?" Benji suddenly looked nervous. "Besides me, I mean. I know the garage code, but I would never—"

"Relax, Benji. I know you wouldn't." I bit my lip. "I have a friend that knows it, too. He was here earlier, dropping off some test results on Dust for me. Test results that are now missing, along with anything else I may have had related to the case."

I had already called Frankie and bitched him out bitterly. I had the phone on speaker while Howell cleaned my arm and I chewed over-the-counter pain pills. It wasn't Frankie's fault, of course, but I needed someone to vent to and Frankie was always good at listening.

"Anyone that heard me discussing the garage code with my friend this morning would have learned how to enter my home without leaving any sign or alerting the neighbors."

Benji nodded slowly, his eyes widening in understanding. "Which is why you think there's an inside man."

"Can you think of anyone that may have been monitoring the comm line?"

He shook his head. "No. I wasn't even paying attention to it that closely. I only connected to it when Ross left the office for an errand and I knew I could talk to you without him finding out right away."

"So you haven't been keeping Ellis in the know all day?" Howell asked.

Benjamin shook his head. "Nah, course not. Ross has me on desk duty for the next three months. For following a superior's order." The last bit he said with a pointed look in my direction.

Ouch.

"Sorry, Benji. You didn't deserve that."

Benji shrugged. "I don't really mind. Gives me time to catch up on my podcasts while I do paperwork. And I'm less likely to be shot at." He took another survey of the living room. "What do you want to do about this? And Mrs. Hatterly's call? She says she heard screaming and what may have been gunshots."

"Mrs. Hatterly," I said with a fond sigh. "I love that old bat. Tell her I was doing one of those exercise videos from the internet and got pissy."

We left the mess in the house for Future Ava to take care of. I had to swap my tennis shoes for a pair of sling-back clogs. I couldn't get my swollen ankle in the tennis shoes. At least the pain meds were working, and I could ask my mother to drop by a tub of her secret healing ointment in the morning. It was some blend of herbs I knew almost nothing about and a little splash of motherly affection that would heal my ankle faster than anything a mundane doctor could prescribe. And it smelled nice.

Benji left after speaking to Mrs. Hatterly. He assured me that no other calls had been made about the noise and possible gunshots from my house.

Howell drove—I couldn't ride the Blackbird with only one fully functioning arm—and I gave directions.

"You sure you want to do this tonight?" Howell asked.

"It has to be tonight. Or we lose our chance."

"And do you think Officer Jackson was telling the truth?"

I thought for a moment. "I've known Benji for a long time. We went to school together. We decided to go to the academy together. And the only reason he's not a detective is that he doesn't want the extra responsibility. He's happy being my partner and letting me take the top spot on Ross's shit list."

"That doesn't answer my question."

"I think it does."

Howell pulled to a stop only feet from where I had parked my bike a few hours before. Freya was locking up her shop, but stopped when I opened the door and stepped carefully out.

"Hi, Ava!" She beamed at me, eying the sling on my arm. "I was hoping you would come back. You forgot your candle."

Howell stepped out of the car and around the hood. "Need a hand, Maxwell?"

I waved Howell off. "Freya, I actually came back to see if you could help me out again."

"Of course." She extended a hand to Howell. "I take it you're one of Ava's partners? You have a really nice aura."

Howell shook her hand. "Thanks."

I pulled the talisman from the inside of my sling. I caught a lovely whiff of my own sweat as I held it out for Freya. Man, I wanted a shower. And food. And sleep.

"I caught it. It wasn't quite as easy as you made it out to be."

Freya glared at me, taking the talisman from my hand. "I remember very specifically saying that you were insane for trying, and that if you survived I would love to take you out for dinner."

My neck warmed. Howell blinked.

Freya inspected the stone in the talisman. "He's strong, for a minor demon."

"That's a minor demon?" Howell and I both asked at the same time.

Freya nodded, still staring at the stone. It was no longer a translucent white, but had grown darker and occluded. "My talisman wouldn't have been able to hold a major demon. I don't have the talent to make something strong enough to house something like that, even for a few hours."

"So it's really in there?" Howell asked. "That big ugly-dog-looking thing?"

"Mhm. Until midnight, I would guess." Freya unlocked the door to her shop and held the door open for us.

"What happens at midnight?" Howell asked. "It just gets out again?"

"The summoning should end at midnight, right?" I asked.

"It should, if your summoner is following proper protocols for summoning an entity like this." Freya locked the door behind us, leaving only the interior shop lights on. "After midnight, the demon will be returned to the Nether until he is summoned again."

"The Nether?" Howell asked.

"Super scary demon plane. Like an alternate dimension inside our own. Full of big ugly things like that guy." I pointed at the talisman.

"That's one theory, yes. Another theory is that it's home to all sorts of creatures, not just demons. And that it's just a tiny pocket of empty space alongside our own. If you open the pocket and call, you can summon forth a number of different creatures."

I had never heard that theory before.

"So, what do we do with that thing until midnight?" Howell asked.

"We use it to find the summoner, and hopefully close this Dust case tonight."

Freya passed the talisman back to me. "It certainly has enough energy to make the casting work."

She led us back to the checkout counter, where a huge book lay open. The cover was a different color than the one Freya had searched through before, and the pages were still a fresh and crisp cream color rather than the aged yellow of the other. There was also a map of the metro printed out and spread out along the counter. It was about six pages in total and covered from as far north as Edmond to as far south as Noble. It was a straight line down I-35, with parts of Midwest City to the east and all of Mustang to the west cut off.

"I took the time to get some things prepared, on the off chance you didn't die," Freya said as she walked around to the far side of the counter. "It's actually pretty hard to find a nice map of so much of the metro area without losing the sense of location you need to be super precise with this spell."

"You did great, Freya." I put the talisman on the counter, examining the map. "Now what?"

Freya took the talisman, flipped it over, and smacked

the top few inches hard against the corner of the counter. The gem fell out and into her waiting hand. "Now we get down to business."

I just stared at her. She had no qualms whatsoever when it came to slamming around a chunk of wood with a stone containing a demon.

I'll admit, it was pretty hot.

Control yourself, Ava.

Freya took the quartz stone freed from the talisman and wrapped a thick metal cord around it using quick, corkscrew motions. "Man, are you two lucky I picked up some more jewelry-making supplies yesterday and was too lazy to take it all home."

She pinched the wire off the roll it unspooled from with a few bends to weaken it and a light tug, curled the two ends up together to make a loop, then set the gem aside and knelt to search behind the counter.

I picked up the stone to inspect it. It had taken Freya maybe fifteen seconds to wrap the stone in wire, and it looked so artistic and unlike anything I could ever do in even fifteen minutes. "How did you learn so much about … so much?"

Freya popped back up from behind the counter with a wooden spool of black nylon cording and a pair of silver shears with stylized handles. "My grandma was kind of the arcane equivalent of a renaissance woman. She taught me just about everything I know." She looped a length of nylon over her shoulders and measured out a piece long enough to reach a few inches below her sternum, then cut the cord. "Some herb lore, a huge amount of homeopathy, and, of course," Freya gave me a wink, "business management."

"Sounds like the real deal."

Freya dropped the crystal onto the nylon cord and started making a complicated-looking knot. "The realest. I bet you would have liked her. She probably would have taken on a minor demon like this one and come out about as well as you did."

"I'm flattered."

She dropped the crystal into my hand and looped the nylon around my middle finger. "Have you ever done a spell like this before?"

I shook my head. "Nope."

"Then I'll handle the magic, you just handle the stone." She looked over my shoulder. "And maybe get your partner back over here, he's been staring at my boob candles for a while."

"Howell, over here," I called. I hadn't even noticed him walk away.

He returned to the counter and leaned against it. "Are we ready for the mumbo jumbo magic tricks, then?"

Freya gave Howell a leveled gaze. "Shall I explain the mumbo jumbo for the unenlightened?"

Howell raised an eyebrow and snorted. "Please do."

Freya pointed at the stone. "So, we know there's a minor demon summoned by someone in connection with this case you're working, right? And this demon has been out and about for the better part of a full day, killing people. Am I up to date so far?"

I nodded, and Howell muttered a short, "Yeah."

"I told Ava earlier that the summoning would remain active for twenty-four hours and would be giving off massive amounts of arcane energy during that time."

"So, you're going to use the demon from the summoning to figure out where the energy is being put off," Howell said, "because they're on the same energy wavelength or whatever." He pointed at the papers on the counter. "Hence the maps."

Freya smiled at him. "You're not as unenlightened as

you look, Howell." She took my hand and gently pulled it until it hovered over the center of her map. Her hand was warm. "It's not exactly like that. All arcane energy functions at roughly the same wavelength, if we're using scientific terms. In fact, it falls typically in the three-hundred-and-thirty to three-hundred-and-fifty nanometer range, meaning arcane energy is actually a form of UVA radiation." Freya opened my palm and turned my hand over, letting the crystal fall and be suspended over the map. "Which is why it's very important to make sure you apply sunscreen before doing any large arcane work."

I blinked. "What?"

She clicked her tongue disapprovingly. "It seems you still have a lot to learn about the arcane, Ava."

"Is that why cats are the most common familiar for witches?" Howell asked. "Because they can see UV light and react to it?"

Freya gave him a surprised look. "You are correct." She shrugged. "And because cats are awesome."

Howell crossed his arms sheepishly. "Yeah, but dogs are pretty awesome, and they can also see UV light. I don't know why it's gotta be cats—"

"Because dogs, bless their little hearts, react to every-thing." Freya put a hand on her hip. "If your dog barks, you have no way of knowing if it's because he heard something five blocks away or if it's because someone is aiming an arcane sniper shot at your head."

"Yeah, but cats—"

"Hey," I shouted. I snapped the fingers of my free hand a few times. And then winced from the pain in my arm where the demon had cut me open. "We can continue this argu-ment later." My arm was beginning to tire from being held up for so long. "Demon in the gemstone, murderous arcanist somewhere in the metro, I almost died like two hours ago. Any of this ringing any bells for you two?"

"Right." Freya gave Howell one last sideways glance as she lifted my hand another inch higher. "The important thing is that, yes, I will be using the demon sealed in the gemstone to give us a fairly accurate location for the arcanist that summoned him. The spell itself is pretty straightforward. Just a variation on a typical seeking spell."

"Oh, I could have done that," I said.

"How accurate are we talking here?" Howell asked.

Freya's head tilted as she thought for a second. "Down to a quarter of a mile, perhaps? We'll have to bring out smaller maps and repeat the spell to get major streets and city blocks, but what's already here will be good enough to start with."

A quarter mile? That's impressive.

"You ready?" Freya asked me.

Only one small edge of the gemstone was touching the map printouts, and it shook slightly with the light tremble in my hand. I nodded. "Let's do it quickly before my arm falls off."

Freya put a hand over mine, her palm barely touching the back of my hand. She closed her eyes. One of her eyelids had a tiny reddish-brown freckle near the outer corner.

I had never done an arcane working with someone before, and it was strange feeling someone else's energy building up so close to me. There was a strange metallic taste in my mouth. I glanced in Howell's direction as he took a quiet step back from us. He had an uncomfortable expression on his face.

I could sympathize. It definitely felt weird.

I went back to watching Freya. I could see her eyes moving slowly under her eyelids, and her lips were parted slightly. She was taking deep, steadying breaths and letting each out slowly. Her breath smelled faintly of something minty. Gum, maybe.

"Maxwell," Howell said.

I looked at him, but his eyes were on the papers spread between Freya and me.

I looked down at the gemstone. It had moved several inches away from me, just enough to pull gently on the nylon cord. It was moving north, following roughly the same path as the interstate. When it stopped, it was settled right over central Oklahoma City.

"Looks like I didn't need to be quite so inclusive with my map," Freya said. She lifted her hand from mine. "Shall I ready another set to narrow down the search?"

Howell tapped on his cell phone, which sat on the counter a hand's breadth from the maps. "Why not use a phone and one of those map apps? Then you can just zoom in every few seconds instead of wasting paper?"

Freya blinked very slowly.

"Smart, Howell." I patted him on the back, then pulled my own cell phone out of my back pocket. "But we'll use my phone. I need you to call in the troops."

Howell nodded. "Alright."

"But do it quietly," I emphasized. "I don't want even a whiff of this to reach anyone at APD."

"Not even Ross?" Howell said, arching an eyebrow.

I thought of the symbol on my door. Someone at APD was working with Mr. Hook, and I couldn't help but wonder if it could be my own commander.

"Especially not Ross."

TWELVE

Howell and I spent another two hours getting everything ready. With Freya's help, we were able to narrow the search radius down to half a mile. From there, it was easy enough to tie a simplified version of Freya's tracking spell to the quartz stone. I watched her work, memorizing the steps she took. It was very similar to tracking work I had done in the past. It was made a little more complex by the fact that the item she was binding the spell to contained a pissed-off demon, but that really just meant it would tire the user a little faster than usual.

The user, of course, being me.

Freya didn't let me leave without giving me a warning. "Just remember not to let it tire you out completely. That last thing you need on top of your injuries is a bout of arcane sickness."

She was right. But I would live with arcane sickness if it meant making a huge Dust bust.

While Freya and I worked to get the demon stone turned into a makeshift arcane compass, Howell called in the calvary. He made a number of calls, talking in hushed tones to a few and loudly reminding another that he was owed a favor. When it was all said and done, he promised we would have plenty of backup and gear at our disposal.

I rode with Howell again, and for the third time in less than twenty-four hours, I found myself in the parking garage across from Club 405.

The club had not been reopened yet, and the parking garage was mostly empty. It was too late in the day for much employee parking and too early in the evening for those same spots to be filled with partiers.

Howell and I took the elevator up to the roof of the garage while the SWAT team geared up. He followed me around patiently as I paced the mostly empty rows of cars, the demon's stone hanging loosely from my hand.

"Anything?" Howell asked.

"Maybe." There was a gentle tug on the nylon cord, and I followed the direction the stone pointed in. My stomach cramped, and a wave of nausea made me pause long enough to fight down the sudden urge to vomit.

"You alright?"

"Yeah, stomach rumbled," I lied.

"We get these guys and get them downtown," Howell started, "I'll take you for some midnight tacos before I get you home. Sound good?"

"Tacos ..." I almost salivated with the word. "That sounds so good."

I kept walking, following the gentle tug of the demon stone. It led me to the far northwest corner of the parking garage roof, and I looked out across the streets. It seemed quiet from five floors above the ground. I heard a piano playing down the street, likely through an outdoor sound system.

"It's coming from over there." I pointed a few blocks

away at a building some ten to twelve stories high only a mile or so from the Devon tower.

"The American Banjo Museum?" Howell asked skeptically.

"Wha— no, Howell. The big fucking building I'm pointing at."

"Right." He stood beside me, surveying the streets below. "I'll send a pair of officers over to talk to the security guards and get the layout for the building. And a list of the businesses that have office space inside."

"Good." I sat down on the parking garage floor.

"Is that a police station just down the street?"

"I noticed that."

"You mean these assholes have been working right under our noses this whole time?"

I rested my head against the concrete barricade and closed my eyes. "You can't blame them. These guys aren't some little street gang. They're working above a bank, for crying out loud."

"You okay, Maxwell?" Howell knelt beside me, putting a hand on my shoulder.

"I'm fine. Just really damn tired."

It wasn't a complete lie. I hadn't slept in almost two days, and I was reaching my limit. But I could also feel sweat breaking out on my forehead and an intense pressure behind my eyes. I had come perilously close to draining myself of arcane energy, and it had taken less than five minutes. I seriously needed some good rest.

I stood up, using the barricade to help me to my feet. "Alright, get your guys moving and then help me gear up."

"You sure you want to go in there? You look like you're going to pass out."

"I've got more in me than you think. I just need some help with the Kevlar."

Howell preceded me down the stairs, grabbing the first two officers he could find that didn't quite look ready to bust down a drug gang and sent them to the building I had pointed out. They took a black SUV, and half a dozen fully kitted officers crammed themselves into the back and went along for the ride.

I opened the trunk to Howell's car and pulled out an extra vest he had packed just for me. I pulled it on awkwardly over the sling and waited for Howell to come and tighten the thing up for me. I briefly wondered how I was going to dress myself for the next few days, and decided that was tomorrow's problem.

Howell tightened the Velcro straps that held the vest on, giving me another chance to back out and stay behind. "I know you like the heated seats in the sedan. You can't pretend you don't."

"The heated seats will still be there when we finish this." I tugged my hair from the shoulder straps of the vest and pulled at the topmost row of Velcro. It pinched my underarm slightly. I hated wearing Kevlar. "One more favor, if you don't mind?"

"Sure."

I pulled an elastic hairband from my pocket. "You ever do a ponytail?"

Howell laughed. "Believe it or not, yes."

I turned my back to him and let him pull my hair out of my face. "Was it your man bun phase in college?"

"I have a niece. She's six."

"Huh. I didn't peg you for the uncle type." I touched the little updo he had given me. It was messy, but it would hold. "You're a little too uptight."

Howell gave me a wounded look. "I take offense. You've yet to see my weekend form."

"Detective!"

Howell and I both turned. An officer in a vest and heavy boots approached. He had a headset over one ear.

"We have the floor plans and resident list."

"And?" Howell asked.

"Bank on the first three floors and the basement, all offices there are empty. Various small companies and a large shared workspace on the next four floors, all being emptied now. Eight and ninth floors closed for remodeling, and the top two floors are owned by a pharmaceutical company. They still have several employees present."

Howell gave me a look. "Pharmaceutical company?"

I nodded, remembering Frankie's talk of isomers and whatever else from that morning. "Sounds promising."

"Freight elevator?"

"In the back, sir. Stops at the tenth floor."

Howell nodded. "We use the freight elevator and do a floor-by-floor survey."

The officer rushed off, pressing the headset to his ear and barking a few orders.

"You do realize they're probably going to be armed?" I asked.

"So are we."

"And there's a sorcerer among them. Someone stronger than me on a good day. And today has not been a good day."

Howell nodded. "I know. SWAT will take care of the bad guys with the guns. You and I will work on the sorcerer. Alright?"

I gave him a one-shoulder shrug. "Alright. Let's get it."

We took a total of three vehicles over to the building. One was another black SUV with about eight guys inside. A van with equipment I didn't think we would need and another four guys followed exactly one minute behind. And finally, Howell and I took his black sedan and parked at the side of the building, in a loading zone, to be precise. I opened my mouth to make a snide comment to Howell, but he beat me to it.

"I'm loading your tired ass in and out of the car. It counts."

"Fair enough."

Two young adults, one male and one female, exited the building's side entrance as we entered. They both had backpacks over their shoulders, and one had a laptop with a charging cord dangling from it pressed to her chest. They looked scared shitless. And then I noticed the entire first floor was swarming with SWAT, and it became clear why.

I made a quick head count.

Yep, twenty officers decked out in full combat uniform is probably enough to scare a regular citizen.

The officer with the headset approached. "All floors but the top two have been cleared. We're prepared to do a second sweep and begin evacuating the remaining floors."

"No," I said, stepping to stand beside Howell. "Those top two floors have got to be the guys we're after."

Howell nodded. "She's right. We'll split into teams." He pointed to the double row of elevators lining the entrance. "Get these shut down. I don't want anyone using them. One team takes the front stairs, one team takes the back. I need six with me on the freight elevator."

"Yes, sir."

"We take each floor and do a ninety-second sweep. Got that?" Howell waited for the officer to nod. "I don't want to give these guys the chance to realize we're here."

I did more quick mental math.

Ninety seconds a floor, nine floors and a basement, that's—

"Too long," I said. "Fifteen minutes is too long to wait."

Howell gave me a reassuring look. "It'll go by a lot faster than you think, trust me."

An overweight security guard ran up to the officer in the headset. "I got the elevators shut down, and the security lockouts for the doors have been disabled."

Howell nodded to the officer in the headset. "You're on point for this one, Morgan. I have a PI consultant to babysit."

A PI consultant?

"Babysit?" I protested.

Howell ignored me, addressing the security officer instead. "What do you know about the pharmaceutical company at the top of the building?"

The man shrugged. "Not much. They work long hours. Have a lot of employees. The owner seems nice. He's got an accent. He brings me donuts every Saturday."

"English accent?" I asked.

The security officer nodded. "Yeah."

"He got a name?" Howell asked.

"Seymour something," the security guard said. "It should be on that list I printed for your guys."

"Seymour Hobbs, owner of Hobbs Manufacturing Services," headset guy, Morgan, said, reading over a list on a clipboard.

I made a face. "Seymour? Yeah, definitely not American. He would have been laughed out of every school in the state."

"I had a great uncle named Seymour," Howell said. He reached for the clipboard and rifled through the pages. There were several pages of blueprints, and he pointed out the ones for the top two floors for me. "Have the first floor and basement already been cleared and searched?"

Both the security guard and Morgan nodded.

"Guess what, Maxwell? We just shaved three minutes off." Maxwell offered the clipboard to me, and I took it. "Let's go."

I followed behind him, surprised to have six SWAT offi-cers instantly circle the pair of us, Morgan included. We stepped into the freight elevator and Howell pressed the buttons for all the first nine floors. He nodded to Morgan, who pressed a button on his earpiece and made some sharp commands into the mouthpiece.

Howell leaned close to me and spoke quietly into my ear. "See if you can figure out where this summoning might be taking place. If some part of those plans might be better suited to it or something. If we get there fast, we can arrest the one responsible for Feldman's murder." He pulled out his weapon, a standard-issue handgun, and held it pointed down.

"And Tooms's. And the club bouncer's." I studied the plans for the tenth floor. I'd never tried reading blueprints before, and it took me a second to make sense of them.

"Yeah. And Ginny could have been killed, if you hadn't made the connection between the symbol and murders."

"And I could be on that list too, if you hadn't shown up like you did, gun blazing." The elevator door dinged, and the six officers with us exited with weapons half raised. Howell and I waited to one side of the elevator, and Howell propped the door open with his foot. "So, thanks."

"No problem. I hope you would have done the same for a fellow officer."

I refrained from making a comment about handling it much more intelligently than he had, and instead only gave a tired shrug. "How is Ginny?"

"Still at the station. I called her foster family before leaving your girlfriend's shop. They didn't seem surprised that she was in trouble with the law."

I ignored the comment about Freya and focused instead on the news about Ginny. "Ouch."

"I told them she was staying with us for her own safety, and that she would be released in the morning."

"How did Ginny take it?" I asked.

"Oh, she was pissed."

"Better pissed off than dead."

The SWAT team filed in once more. "Empty," Morgan said.

"Alright, next floor," Howell said. He let the door shut, then pushed me into the corner behind him.

I rolled my eyes and studied the blueprints. The tenth floor was basically just a square. The center was completely empty, meaning none of the normal elevators made it that high in the building. The freight elevator was on the north side of the building while the stairs were on the east and west sides. From the center of the floor, there seemed to be a sort of lobby by the west stairs. And the entire south wall and roughly half of the east wall were all one long hallway with three long rooms and a third set of stairs.

"This is weird." I pointed out the third set of stairs to Howell, then flipped to the floor plan for the top floor. "These stairs are the only way to the top floor. And they're probably behind a locked door."

Howell frowned. "What about roof access?"

I checked the blueprints. "The other stairs will get you to the roof, but they bypass the eleventh floor entirely."

"What do you think that means?"

"It means we have a weird bottleneck to get to the top floor." I examined the blueprints closer. The top floor was a single large room. "And I bet that's where we need to go."

The elevator dinged again, and everyone but Howell and I filed out.

"Alright, so we let SWAT clear a path for us to those stairs." Howell pressed a hand against the freight elevator doors to once more keep them from shutting. It pressed me further into the corner. "You've got about ten minutes left to just rest and reload. You gonna be okay?"

"I will be if you gave me a little more breathing room." I pushed on his back, putting maybe three inches between my nose and the gap between Howell's shoulder blades. "You don't seriously buy that babysitting shit, do you?"

"Hey, you've been playing little witch woman all day. This is what I'm good at." Howell still held his gun pointed at the elevator floor. "Let me do my job."

"I'll be fine."

"You're unarmed and exhausted."

The officers filed back in again. "One still in an office in the back. He's being escorted to the lobby."

Howell nodded. "Alright. Let's keep moving."

THIRTEEN

The remainder of the elevator ride was quiet and grim. Howell seemed quite comfortable, and I briefly wondered how many similar buildings he had stormed during his time as a detective. With each stop on the floors leading up to the top of the building, Howell held the door open while his men streamed out and quickly set out to secure the floor. I occasionally spotted members of the other two teams taking the stairs, but each group stayed fairly close to their entrance and exit point.

We all paused as the door closed after clearing the ninth floor. It was being renovated, as Morgan had mentioned earlier, and there were ladders and buckets of tools. Two men in paint-splattered overalls speaking rapid Spanish were guided to the stairs and told to exit the building.

The elevator doors muffled the upbeat music playing from a Bluetooth speaker balanced on a step stool, and my anxiety instantly went up a notch.

"How many can we expect to find on the top two floors?" Morgan asked Howell.

Howell looked over his shoulder at me, but I could only give a one-shoulder shrug.

"I dunno. Might be one. Might be a hundred."

Morgan frowned and gave Howell a displeased look.

"Just tell me when your men are in place."

Morgan repeated the order over the headset. There was approximately ten seconds of silence, followed by two brief cracks of static and faint murmuring from Morgan's earpiece. He nodded at Howell. "Ready."

Howell pressed the button for the tenth floor, and the elevator began its final ascent.

I took a deep breath and held it.

Morgan's finger hovered over the button on his headset.

Weapons were lifted as the elevator slowed.

The elevator dinged, and Howell pressed me further into the corner.

"Now," Morgan said into his mic.

The doors to the freight elevator opened and shouts instantly went up as Morgan and his men exited.

I heard a woman's startled scream and the sound of glass shattering. Howell waited a few seconds and then stepped from the elevator. I took the chance to follow him, tossing the clipboard with the blueprints into the elevator as the door shut behind me.

I had assumed that the tenth floor would be walls and locked doors. The blueprint had made the entire floor seem like it was designed to be very closed off and secretive.

I had been very wrong.

On exiting the elevator, the first thing I saw were long glass windows from about waist height to perhaps two feet below the ceiling. The window wrapped along the south wall and to the eastern stairwell, where SWAT members were leading men and women in white lab coats, goggles, and covered shoes back down to the first floor.

At least I had been right about the lobby area, though it was more of a small break room than a true lobby. There were a pair of vending machines and some tables and chairs set up, and a man in jeans and a plaid fleece button-up lying on his stomach with his hands on the back of his head.

"Maxwell." Howell turned to me. "I was expecting men with guns. Not men with beakers." He pointed through one of the windows, where SWAT members were leading more scientist-looking figures out. "What the hell is this?"

I could only stare at the various instruments and equipment in the rooms. "I don't know."

There was a commotion as Morgan led a man in a crisp white lab coat out of one of the labs.

"Unhand me, you Neanderthal! I want your badge number. And your superior's badge number."

Howell and I approached as the man continued to berate Morgan. His face was turning an amusing shade of red, and he slapped ineffectually at Morgan's helmet.

"Morgan, bring him here," Howell said.

The scientist tugged his arm free of Morgan's slackened grip and turned on Howell. "How dare you storm into my laboratory and drag us out like common criminals!"

"What the hell is this place, if you don't mind me asking?" Howell waved a finger around to indicate the glass-enclosed labs. "They look like clean rooms."

"They *were* clean rooms until you idiots paraded through," the man said. "This is a privately owned medical manufacturing company."

"And what is it that you're manufacturing?" Howell asked.

The man sneered. "The exact nature is proprietary, and I doubt you would understand the complexities of it anyway. But it is a new pain-management medication currently being researched and in the process of beginning human trials."

"So, not street drugs?" I asked. Stupidly, I'll add. I asked stupidly, and with great confusion.

The man scowled. "No, of course not."

"May I see a sample of the drug you're manufacturing?" Howell asked.

I pulled Howell away from the pissed-off scientist even as he began shouting protestations. "There isn't time. We can figure out what this is after we clear the top floor."

"You think they might be making Dust here, and passing it off as a pain medicine?" Howell asked in a hushed tone.

"I don't know. Maybe they are making a new medicine. Or maybe they *think* they are."

Howell gestured to Morgan. "Get him downstairs. We'll finish clearing the building and then figure out what the hell is going on here."

"When I inform Mr. Hobbs what's happened, I'm sure he will have your jobs."

"Oh, good. I'd like to talk to Mr. Hobbs myself," I asked. "Where can I find him?"

The scientist frowned. "I would assume he's still in his office, up on the next floor."

"Great, thanks." I gave Morgan a thumbs up. "Now you can take him downstairs." I slapped Howell on the shoulder. "You're with me, boss man."

Howell gave a sharp whistle, and five SWAT members with no detained chemists to guide down the stairs followed Howell's motion to move on the stairs leading to the eleventh floor. They took the lead, Howell right at their heels, and I charged up behind them at a much more sedate pace. The pain medication I had taken earlier was already wearing off, and my clogs were not the best for running up stairs. But I booked it as fast as I could.

The stairs were broad and carpeted, with very nice

wooden balustrades that I used to help me haul my ass up to the top floor. And at the top was a set of wooden doors with the name Seymour Hobbs in vinyl appliqué in a very gauche font across both doors.

It looked terrible and very much like something a video-game hero might encounter before a final boss fight.

I felt a wave of lightheadedness descend on me as I reached the top.

Damn arcane sickness. At least let me get through the night.

I was going to have to work on my arcane stamina. How, I had no idea. But it was going to happen.

Howell put a hand on the doorknob and tested it. It turned slightly in his hand, and he nodded at the men clustered in the doorway. He shoved me to the side and swung the door open.

The SWAT team poured in like black liquid. Orders were immediately shouted for someone to get to their knees with their hands raised, and Howell and I both stepped inside. Howell held his gun at his side and kept me behind him.

The room stank of arcane energy like there had been an active thunderstorm focused in the room only moments before, along with the sharp undertone of aerosolized sunblock. It was an unmistakable smell that brought to mind hot summers by the pool.

And there was a big fucking symbol painted on the floor in the center of the room in red paint. I didn't even need to get a close look at it to know it was the same symbol that Howell and I had been seeing all day. With one exception. There was a black X painted over it. It all looked to be done in actual paint, and I spotted a half-gallon pail with a few red drippings against one wall.

Seymour Hobbs, if I had to guess at his identity, was standing in the center of the symbol with his back to us and his arms raised. He had lightly tanned skin and salt-and-pepper hair that looked expensive to maintain, and wore a very nice fitting grey suit. I had been expecting another lab coat. Or perhaps a red crushed-velvet cloak.

The SWAT team circled him, and I felt a surge of energy as one of them reached for an upraised hand to bring him down.

"Howell, down!" I shoved Howell hard and dove to the ground. We both landed on our knees, and the only reason I didn't face plant was that I fell into Howell's shoulder with my injured arm.

My howl of pain was drowned out by the sound of five bodies slamming into the walls around us as Hobbs let out a radiating blast of arcane energy.

"Shit," Howell said. He rose to his feet, gun pointed at Hobbs, and fired two shots at his back.

Neither hit Hobbs. Or anything, for that matter.

Hobbs summoned a shield and stopped the bullets mid-flight. They hovered, two tiny little pieces of metal, in a strange gelatinous shield the likes of which I had never seen.

Hobbs turned with slow, purposeful steps and stopped to face me. "Maxwell. I was hoping you would make it."

His accent was the sexiest damn English accent I had ever heard in my entire life.

Howell kept his gun upraised. "Maxwell, what's the plan?"

I have no idea, man.

I was too stunned to speak.

"I was surprised when you managed to survive my demon. And I'm even more surprised to realize that you captured it." Hobbs took several steps to one side, stepping out of the symbol's circle. "I assumed you had only banished it from your home when your friend here tarnished the mark I used. I've spent the last few hours thinking he was still out there." Hobbs shrugged. "Silly me."

"You're under arrest, Hobbs." My voice sounded weak. "Now, tell me where the Dust is."

Hobbs raised an eyebrow and smiled. It was a polite and political sort of smile. "Oh, you haven't figured it out yet?" He raised a hand, and I felt another surge of arcane power building. "No matter." He winked at me. "Goodbye, Maxwell."

Hobbs flexed his hand, and I shut my eyes, not sure what to expect and positive I had no way to counter anything he threw at me.

I hit the ground, something heavy and smelling faintly of aftershave on top of me.

"Shit, I've been hit."

It was Howell, and I opened my eyes to see the side of his face uncomfortably close.

"Nice pores, asshole. Now get off me." And then what he'd said clicked. "What do you mean hit?"

Howell slid off me, and I looked up to see Hobbs giving the ceiling a hard stare. With another, smaller surge of arcane power, Hobbs disappeared.

"I mean that English prick shot me with my own bullets." Howell groaned, tugging at the Velcro that held his vest on. "Two in the back, both caught by the vest." He gasped, a pained expression on his face. "Right in the lung. It'll hurt to breathe for so long."

I tore at the Velcro to pull the vest off. "Hobbs is on the roof. Teleportation spell, just like Tooms said."

Howell shoved at my hand, pushing me away. "Go get him."

"What the hell am I supposed to do against that guy?"

"Use your special talents." Howell slid his gun my way.

"Try shooting him again. Shove him off the building. I don't care."

"Did you really just take a couple of bullets for me, Howell?"

Howell gave me a nasty look. "Get to the roof, Maxwell!"

"Right." I stood awkwardly, then bent to retrieve Howell's gun. "We can do the emotional shit later."

I went back the way we'd come, jogging down the stairs, my injured arm bouncing painfully.

"No big deal. Just me, with a busted-up arm and no arcane energy left, going up against the strongest arcanist I have ever met, with nothing more than a gun with two spent rounds."

The tenth floor was empty. The men and women in lab coats were gone, the SWAT team with them. I took the closest set of stairs, yanking open the door awkwardly, and almost slammed in Morgan.

"Where's Howell? I heard gunshots."

"Eleventh floor. He took two in the vest."

"Shit." Morgan slipped around me, giving me an ugly glare.

Whatever. I had bigger concerns than making some guy my friend. And he would help stupid, stubborn Howell get back on his feet and into a new vest.

I charged up the stairs, taking them two at a time and enunciating every other step with a small *ow* of pain. I paused at the roof exit, taking a deep breath before pushing the metal door open and stepping out onto the paved roof.

Hobbs was some thirty feet away, waiting for me. I brought Howell's gun up and aimed it at Hobbs.

He was unarmed. Or at least wasn't holding any obvious mundane weapons. But that energy blast had been far more powerful than anything I could have conjured and I had no idea how much he still had in him.

"Alright, Hobbs." I stepped closer, angling my approach so I could easily dive behind a nearby AC unit. "You ready to come along? Or do we need to have ourselves a little old-school throw down?"

Hobbs laughed. "I have no plans to quarrel with you, Miss Maxwell. It would be a waste of my time, honestly."

That pissed me off. "Look here, fucker." I kept my gaze leveled on him and stood my ground. "That was a little insulting. How about you apologize and get on your knees before I shoot you?"

Hobbs lifted an eyebrow and smiled that pleasant little smile. "In this suit? I think not."

"Hands up and on your knees, Hobbs," I said.

He lifted his hands, but only up to shoulder height. "Please, call me Seymour. I think a few failed murder attempts can permit us first-name basis. Wouldn't you agree, Ava?"

"You think you can freak me out by telling me you know my name?" I laughed. "I already know there's a rat in the APD."

"Oh, Ava, darling." He winked at me again. His eyes were a rich honey color that matched his skin tone nicely. "I've known about you for a bit longer than that."

I shrugged, ignoring the protest from my shoulder. "Then let's take this conversation back to an interrogation room. Maybe get to know each other a little better."

The door behind me burst open. The metal slammed against the frame with an echoing clatter than made me jump.

"That you, Howell?" I called over my shoulder. I didn't want to look away from Hobbs for even a second.

"It's me." Howell was already at my back, and I shifted

to give him space to share my cover. "I brought a little help."

I relaxed when I saw Morgan taking up a position to my right behind another AC unit. His weapon was up and trained on Hobbs, but Hobbs took no notice of the additional manpower.

"Tell your father I said hello, Ava." Hobbs backtracked several steps, bringing himself closer to the roof's edge. Morgan followed, shouting for him to stop moving and get to his knees.

My stomach dropped. So did my weapon, though only by a few inches.

Hobbs backed up until his thighs met the retaining wall at the roof's edge. He sat, still staring at me. "Until next time." He leaned back, letting himself fall over the edge—he was gone in an instant.

Morgan and Howell both rushed to the retaining wall and looked over. I followed more slowly, my mind numb and refusing to process the last several seconds.

Morgan was speaking rapidly into his headset, and I caught a few words about a body on the ground. He paused, staring over the edge, and I heard faint static as an answer came back to him. Morgan turned to Howell, his head tilted. "Nothing."

Howell turned to me. His brows were knitted together. "He's gone."

I nodded. "Yeah, probably."

"Care to explain, Maxwell?"

I blinked and dared a look over the roof's edge. It was a dizzying height, and I quickly stepped back. "I'm not sure I can."

I passed Howell's gun back to him. "But I don't think that was the last time we'll see him."

CHAPTER

FOURTEEN

"Wow, so this is what a privately operated lab looks like?" Frankie whistled, eying the equipment around him.

"Just tell me what you think, Mr. Alvarez," Howell asked.

I leaned heavily against a wall, watching Frankie explore the room with interest. He was careful not to touch anything, though he had slipped on a pair of blue gloves. Howell had given him a lengthy treatise on the importance of not leaving his fingerprints or even a fallen eyelash on anything in the room.

"I think I might be wasting my time getting a PhD if places like this are hiring." Frankie turned to me. "How much do you think these guys make in a year?"

I shrugged. "Probably not enough to unwittingly be a part of a drug manufacturing scheme."

Frankie stopped at a computer monitor and stared at it for a moment. He clicked a few buttons with the mouse, ignoring the glare from Howell. "Fascinating."

"What is, Mr. Alvarez?"

He looked up at Howell with a pout. "They're running

Windows 10. And their software is updated to the latest version."

"Dammit, Frankie." I closed my eyes, ignoring the nausea that threatened to send me to the nearest bathroom. "I didn't ask you up here so you could get grumpy about the university's research funding."

"I dropped everything to run up here and play science consult for you, Ava. Let me have a little look at what I'm missing in the corporate world."

Frankie reached for a tray of tiny vials, but a shout went up.

"Don't touch those! Those are the property of Hobbs Manufacturing and should not be handled by untrained buffoons."

"Ah, I see Morgan has returned with our mad scientist," I said.

Morgan led the angry gentleman from earlier in by the elbow. His hands were cuffed loosely in front of him, and his lab coat had been removed. He wore a crisp button-up in a medium shade of green with a stain from what might have been mustard on the front.

The man glared at me. "My name is Dr. Jennings. I am the lab manager." He addressed Frankie again. "Young man, do you have any idea what you're playing with there?"

Frankie's head tilted. "Well, I can't be sure, but I think it's a tray of HPLC samples that were about to be run on this instrument here. But I'm an untrained buffoon and definitely not a fellow scientist, so what do I know?" Frankie rolled his eyes and continued his exploring, muttering darkly under his breath.

Dr. Jennings turned a faint shade of red and turned to Howell. "I understand you have some questions."

"I do, yes," I said, drawing his attention away from

Howell. "Have you ever heard of a street drug called Pixie Dust?"

Dr. Jennings shook his head. "Of course not."

I nodded. "And does this scan look familiar to you?" I pulled a report from a green folder in my hands and passed it to him.

Jennings looked the report over, his brows knitting. "This looks like an XRD scan of our drug formulation. Where did you get this?" He looked from me to Howell. "I don't suppose I need to remind you that this is proprietary information?"

I took the report back. "This is actually a scan of Pixie Dust, analyzed by the untrained buffoon over there." I motioned towards Frankie.

Jennings scoffed. "Untrained indeed. That amorphous peak in the center of the graph is clearly indicative of a contaminant in your sample."

Frankie's indistinct muttering grew noticeably louder, but I maintained composure. "So this big blob on this graph is not present in similar scans of your drug?"

"No."

"And the D-isomer concentration of methamphetamine? Is it at twenty percent in your formulation?" Frankie asked.

Jennings gave Frankie a scowl. "How could you know that?"

"It is my belief, Dr. Jennings," I said, once more pulling the lab manager's attention away from the increasingly frustrated Frankie, "that someone is taking your drug and altering the structure somehow. And then selling it as a street drug."

"Impossible." Jennings shook his head. "Our manufacturing is tightly controlled. We have three shifts, each with a designated shift leader responsible for enforcing proper controlled substance procedures. And I'm here for most of the day, every day. We would have noticed if someone was stealing samples or performing unauthorized experiments."

Howell shuffled through a slim stack of papers he held. "So the only time the medication you're formulating leaves the building is when it gets packaged for delivery to the facility running the blind trials?"

Jennings nodded. "And when we send samples out for third-party potency testing."

"Right." Howell shuffled through the papers again. "For every batch of two hundred and fifty, um …" Howell paused, scrutinizing the paper "… dry-form amber vials, you send twenty-five off for lab testing."

"Thirty-five," Jennings corrected.

Howell shook his head. "No, this definitely says twenty-five."

Jennings lifted his chin, his nose in the air. "It's thirty-five. From a flat case of two hundred and fifty vials, I pull three from each corner, four from each of the short sides of the case, five from the long sides of the case, and five from approximately the center of the case." He gave Howell a pretentious glare. "Thirty-five."

Howell showed him the paper he held. "Well, according to the paperwork for the last batch, ten of those vials were never sent out."

Jennings scowled. "What idiot signed such a ridiculous testing request and neglected to account for the correct number of sample vials?"

Howell looked over at me. "Mr. Hobbs."

I could only nod. I was far too tired to express how thrilled I was that we had just determined how Hobbs was skimming the drug for his own use.

We left some time after, letting SWAT and the local

OKPD handle the rest at Hobbs Manufacturing. Howell and I were back in Ross's office a couple of hours after making it back to Norman.

"I was able to get the lab to run an emergency test on the samples we took from the scene. When compared to the samples Maxwell had already submitted with her earlier reports, they were nearly a match." Howell leaned back in his chair, eying Ross closely.

"Nearly a match?" Ross asked. He looked like shit, but then so did Howell and I. It was a little after midnight, and I still hadn't eaten or slept. There was also the worsening bout of arcane sickness threatening to knock me out any minute.

We had taken all the employees from Hobbs Manufacturing Services and driven them two blocks to the nearest Oklahoma City Police Department. We had also pulled paperwork and financial records, all of which were very easy to find. The results were disappointing, but not entirely surprising.

"It looks like the employees were legit. As was the company they worked for. And the drug they were making was indeed in the research stages with a large clinical research organization." Howell took a sip of his coffee. "The differences between it and Dust were minimal, and we determined Hobbs was skimming quantities of the drug and manipulating them somehow to form Dust."

"The medicine they were formulating was basically a cocktail of various narcotics with a good dose of stimulants mixed in. Think hydrocodone and fentanyl with a side of methamphetamine." I gave Howell a side glance, but he only continued to sip at his coffee. "Dust was just the same drug with some arcane energy wrapped around it. And sugar, to make it sweet."

"But we have no way to verify that this Seymour Hobbs

character was the one responsible for the final transformation of the research medication into Dust, correct? Nor were we able to find anyone responsible for the dissemination of Dust." Ross looked directly at me, a scowl on his face. "Because Hobbs got away."

"If by 'got away' you mean he intentionally fell from an eleven-story building and then disappeared before hitting the ground," Howell said, "then yes, Hobbs got away."

"I'm just trying to understand how you could call in the calvary and not take the time to get one little message to me about this big bust, Phil," Ross said. "And I'm also trying to understand how you could storm a mostly empty building with twenty men and still not make an arrest."

"Funny." Howell finished off his coffee and set the empty cup on Ross's desk. "I've been trying to figure out how the lab had never heard of these Dust samples before last night, and who might have erased them from the testing queue."

Ross and Howell had a short stare down. It would have been intimidating if I weren't so fucking pissed off and exhausted.

Ross was the first to look away. "If you have nothing else to add that is not already in your report, Detective Howell, you're dismissed."

Howell stood and buttoned his suit jacket. It was covered in dirt and wrinkled. "Nothing to add. I'll be in the neighborhood, Ellis."

I didn't stand. I knew Ross wasn't finished with me. And I wasn't finished with him either.

Ross waited until the door to his office shut behind Howell. "The lack of an arrest aside, you and Detective Howell did manage to find out not only who was responsible for Feldman's death, but also who was behind Dust." Ross opened a drawer in his desk and removed my badge, handcuffs, and gun. "I think you can have these back."

I shook my head. "No thanks."

Ross raised an eyebrow. "Excuse me?"

I paused for the time it took to draw in a deep breath and debated if what I was about to do was a wise decision.

But I was just too fucking pissed to think on it for more than a few seconds.

"I quit." I shrugged. My arm was still in a sling, though it had been swapped for a proper one rather than one crafted out of tea towels, and the movement stung.

"Why?"

"I'm not an idiot, Ross." I stared at him, wondering how I ever found him to be intimidating. I had taken on a demon less than twelve hours ago, and Ross was nothing in comparison. "You were pretty sloppy. So sloppy, in fact, that I found myself really wondering if I was right to suspect you. Because there was no way you would make so many stupid mistakes if you really were trying to prevent this Dust case from getting solved."

Ross narrowed his eyes at me. "I don't follow."

"You are the rat in the APD. You were the one listening in on my comm line all day. You were the one that learned how to get into my house. You left the symbol on my door and stole the files I had on the case. And you have been there every step of the way to slow down progress on solving this."

Ross stared at me impassively.

"What did Hobbs promise you, Ross?" I felt my face reddening, and I had to fight to keep from shouting at him. "Money, like what you promised Ginny if she left that symbol on Tooms's house? Did you think I wouldn't pull her file before sending her back to her family, only to realize that you had also requested her file only a few days before?"

I leaned forward, propping my good elbow on my knees. "Or did Hobbs promise you power? Seems he's got plenty of it for himself, and it's clear now that you haven't got enough to dry the piss from your d—"

"Enough," Ross shouted.

The air was warm with crackling energy, and I was surprised to realize most of it was coming from me. Even with the arcane sickness, I evidently still had enough juice to fan a small fire.

I relaxed and sat back in my chair.

Ross did the same. He looked undisturbed by the accusations. "You can't prove anything, Maxwell."

"Maybe not." I nodded. "But I can keep an eye on you. And I swear I will bring you down someday, you little bitch."

Ross motioned to the door. "Get out. Don't bother coming to beg for your job back when you realize the mistake you've made."

I left. Benji wasn't at his desk, or I would have stopped to say goodbye. He was probably long gone for the day. I thought of leaving a note, but a quick text in the morning would be just as easy. And less likely to end up in the trashcan at the side of his desk. So I just stormed away.

Howell was waiting in the parking lot for me just as he'd said he would. "Did you do it?"

"Yeah."

"Still worried it was the right move?"

I nodded. "Yeah."

Howell opened the passenger door and ushered me into the car. "Don't be. I think you did the right thing. And you can always come work for the NPD."

We drove and I dozed a little. I woke up when Howell shook me gently.

"Yeah?" I asked groggily, sitting up. We were in a drive-thru.

"I promised you tacos. What do you want?"

Tacos ...

"I'll take one of everything, you magnificent bastard."

Howell helped me clean up the fried chicken from my living room and the papers from my office. We ate off the fast-food wrapper while sitting on my couch.

"I don't think I want to work for the NPD," I said around a mouthful of taco. "No offense, but I want to focus on growing my arcane talents."

Howell wiped his face with a napkin and squirted a packet of hot sauce onto a burrito. "What do you want to do then?"

I set my half-eaten taco aside and gave him a serious look. "I could do consult work with the NPD."

Howell snorted. "The PI thing with Morgan was just a little fib."

"I'm serious, Howell. Do you think I could make that work?"

Howell considered for a moment. "Probably. I would hire you." He took a massive bite of his burrito. "But maybe get a second gig to go with it." He wiped his mouth again, then smirked at me. "Maybe with that Freya woman. She really seemed to enjoy your company." He dropped his burrito and stood, swallowing quickly. "Which reminds me that she gave me something to give to you before we left her store."

He left through the garage, seeing as the front door was busted and pinned shut with a dining room chair. I waited for him to return, finishing my taco and contemplating whether to take a shower before or after sleep. When he returned, he passed me a small box.

I opened it and a pair of waxed breasts pointed up at

me. The wicks were prominently placed where the nipples would be. I nodded. "Of course."

"She asked me to make sure you knew to put in your bedroom for maximum efficacy."

I threw a sauce packet at him. "Thank you, Howell."

"No problem."

We ate in silence for a moment. I had to stop after a few more bites. I could tell anything more would just make me sick. "How long have we known each other now?"

Howell checked his cell phone, reading the time. "About twenty hours."

I groaned. "Seems a lot longer."

"I'll try not to take offense to that."

"You were a great partner today, Howell. I appreciate everything you did."

Howell nodded. "You're welcome. It was nice to work with someone a little different." He squeezed more hot sauce onto another burrito. His hot sauce usage was questionable. No one needed three packets for a single burrito. "You want to talk about what Hobbs said before he disappeared?"

I frowned. "The thing about my dad?"

Howell nodded. "Does your dad know him?"

"My dad died. A long time ago."

"Oh." Howell paused, inches from taking a massive bite of food. "I'm sorry."

I shrugged. "It's no big deal. I just don't understand what Hobbs meant."

Howell shrugged, talking around a mouthful of food. "Maybe he was just messing with you." He swallowed, wiping his mouth again. "If Ross really was giving him information from inside APD, he could have told Hobbs about your father."

"Maybe." I pointed at the couch. "You want to crash

here tonight? I know your day has been just as long and terrible as mine."

Howell shook his head and started clearing up food wrappers. "Nah, I need to get home to Janet and the kids."

I laughed. "You're married?"

Howell snorted. "Nah. Janet's my dog."

"And the kids?"

He flushed and gave me a warm smile. "She's going to have babies in a few weeks. Vet says she's got six little puppies squirming around."

I laughed. "Congrats, Howell. You're going to be a grandpa."

We tossed our trash and made for the garage.

"I'm taking tomorrow off. I'll come by and check on you. I think you and I both know you overdid it today with the mumbo jumbo witchy stuff."

I rolled my eyes. But honestly, it felt nice to have someone other than my mother worrying about me. "You've got my number, partner."

Howell bounced his keys in the palm of his hand, giving me a serious look. "Get some rest, okay? You look like shit."

"Same to you."

I showered after he left, tossing the sling aside and doing a few minor stretches after the hot water had loosened some of my sore muscles. I had a lot of bruising. It looked like I had definitely taken a couple of beatings. The black eye Feldman had given me was still very prominent under the foundation and glamor I had applied, and I made another mental note to ask my mother about her special cream recipe. It probably had something ridiculous in it, like dandelions plucked under a waning gibbous moon or something similarly annoying to collect.

Maybe Freya knew something about healing blemishes and bruises with arcane talents.

She does have very nice skin …

I thought of texting her, then remembered the only number I had for her was the shop number listed on the internet.

"Another problem for tomorrow."

I checked the front door, making sure the dining room chair would hold through the night, and added "Fix front door" to the growing list of concerns for Future Ava.

And then I fell asleep, and in my sleep, I dreamt.

"Ava, help me get your brother out of his car seat."

"Tell your father I said hello, Ava."

BONUS CONTENT!

Thank you for reading *Settling Dust*, and I hope you enjoyed it. As a special bonus, I've added a bonus short story detailing Ava Maxwell on her first freelancing case.

Keep reading to enjoy *Odd Jobs, Volume One*.

The Maxwell Chronicles
Short Stories

Odd Jobs
Volume One

ODD JOBS

"Wake up, Maxwell. I brought donuts and coffee."

I cursed into my pillow and rolled out of bed. My knees nearly buckled underneath me, but they carried me well enough to the bathroom. I could hear Howell in the kitchen, banging shit around. The kitchen tap ran briefly, and there was the rustling of paper bags.

I called through the closed bedroom door as I dressed. "When you said you would be coming by today, I didn't think it would be first thing in the morning, Howell."

"It's past noon," he called back with a laugh. "I came by first thing this morning, but left when I heard your lovely snores and decided to let you sleep more."

I tugged an oversized tee over my head and wrangled my still very sore left arm through the sleeve without jostling my shoulder any more than necessary. I didn't know whether to be annoyed that Howell—who I had never heard of a few days ago—had now been in my house while I was sleeping twice in the same day, or if I should be touched that he was checking on me. The fact that he had donuts definitely swayed me towards the latter.

I opened the bedroom door and almost tripped over a very large, very pregnant black and brown dog.

"What the—"

Howell turned from the kitchen sink. "Oh sorry, I brought Janet. Hope you don't mind. The vet says I should keep an eye on her. She could pop any minute."

"No, it's fine." I gave the dog a pat on the head. Her fur was very soft, and she wuffed softly and pressed her head deeper into my palm. Her eyes were large and a color somewhere between a deep caramel and a milky chocolate brown. "Hello, Janet."

Janet's tongue lolled, and she turned and waddled off to the back door and sat down. Her belly swayed slightly with each step and forced her to sit with her hind legs at an awkward angle.

"Should I let her outside? The backyard is fenced," I said.

Howell passed me a plate with two chocolate frosted donuts. "I can handle it. Sit and eat something. Freya said fatty foods would be good for you." He gently pushed me towards the dining table, then pulled a chair out for me.

I sat. "When did you talk to Freya? And why are you treating me like an invalid?"

Howell opened the back door long enough for Janet to take herself out into the backyard. "She called me, actually. Dialed the Norman department and got redirected to my work cell."

"And?" I bit into a donut, letting the fried dough and chocolate melt in my mouth a little. Despite the stereotype about cops and donuts, it had been a very long time since my last one.

"And she asked me to check in on you. Told me a little about arcane sickness, and that you were likely to have it." He sat next to me, dropping two cell phones on the table.

"And said she wanted you all fixed up to come see her tomorrow."

I winced. "She's still hung up on a date, huh?" I shook my head. "I don't think she'd want to stick around after a couple of hours with me." I tore the rest of the first donut in half and bit a large piece off, wishing there were more than just two on the plate.

Howell pointed to a paper cup of coffee that I hadn't noticed; a couple of creams and blue sweetener packets lay next to it. "Actually, when I told her you'd quit the APD and were thinking about going into freelance consulting, she said she might have a job for you."

I quickly swallowed and wiped chocolate from my fingers. "That's amazing. Did she say what it was?"

Howell shook his head, tapping away on his phone. "Nah, just to give the shop a call when you were up for it."

I took a breath. "Alright. I'll call her now and head over there soon."

"Nope."

"Nope?" I asked. "What do you mean?"

"Your mother is on her way, and I thought we could spend the day here getting the front door fixed up."

I made a face. "Shit, Howell. You talked to my mother?"

"She called your cell while I was here this morning." He motioned behind me, towards the living room, and I turned to see my cell phone sitting on the coffee table. "I told her about the arcane sickness and that you'd been pretty beat up and needed rest." Howell shrugged. "So she insisted on coming over and taking care of you."

"You didn't tell her about the demon, did you?"

Howell gave me an airy look. "I did not."

"How long do we have until she gets here?"

He lifted the cell phone in his hand to show me a short

text thread. "She just sent me a message saying she's on her way. And that she's bringing more donuts."

Fuck.

"Alright, help me up. I have to clean the house before she gets here or she'll give me hell."

Howell stood and pulled me to my feet. "If it helps, Janet already took care of the fried chicken we missed last night."

I laughed.

Together, Howell and I got the house semi-cleaned. Howell removed the front door, and I was surprised to see that he had already installed a screened-in storm door. In the full light of day, the front entrance didn't look too bad. The door frame and trim would need replacing, but the drywall around it was still mostly intact.

I delegated the heavier tasks to Howell, like organizing the weight rack the demon had knocked over the day before. I hadn't forgotten about the two bullets in the back he had taken the night before, but he made a show of doing a few deadlifts with a forty-five-pound plate in each hand. So I let him do the heavy stuff.

Men are weird.

I did some light cleaning, and quickly worked up a sweat. Janet followed me around loyally. At first I thought it was just because I was a new person and she wanted to familiarize herself with me. Then she let out a single echoing bark as I fought off a dizzy spell. Howell forced me to sit down and drink some water while he took out the trash and sprayed air freshener through the house to hide the stink of demon.

I sipped at a bottle of water while he stood in the kitchen, bent in half so he could rub behind Janet's ears. "So is this the weekend look you mentioned last night?" I motioned at his outfit, a pair of medium-wash jeans that fit slim in the waist and loose in the thighs and calves, and a short-sleeved tee that sat right at the belt line. He even wore a pair of beat-up sneakers, and his hair lacked the styling gel that had been present the day before.

Howell shrugged. "I like to be comfortable when I'm not working." He gave his dog a rough back rub. "And I can't play with my little baby in slacks, can I?"

A car door slammed outside, and my mother's voice drifted in from outside. "Ava, what happened to your door?"

I sighed. "Just doing a little bit of renovation. Nothing to worry about."

My mother is a smaller woman with dark hair, dark eyes, and a stunning ability to always be around when I don't really want her to be. Not to say that I don't love my mother, but over the years she has managed to find the perfect balance between being overly protective and genuinely wonderful in every way a mom could be. It is both fascinating and annoying.

She entered the house, carrying a huge box of donuts and an oversized handbag. "I see you've still got that exercise junk in the front room. I thought you were going to get a nice dining table so you can host nice parties with your friends?"

"I don't have friends, Mom." I stood, taking the donuts from her and setting them on the counter. "*You* thought I was going to get a nice dining table. I like having the exercise junk."

She gave Howell a good look over, one eyebrow heavily arched. "If this one isn't your friend, can I have him?"

"Mom!"

Howell laughed, and they *hugged*. "Nice to meet you, Catherine."

"You too, Phillip. Thanks for telling me about Ava."

I shook my head fiercely. "What wonderland did I just fall into? You're gonna hug a stranger before your own child?"

"Oh, hush, Ava. He sounded handsome on the phone, and I wanted to make sure those muscles were real."

Howell laughed. I gagged. My mother and I embraced. She was wearing perfume, something light and floral. And she had applied a small amount of lipstick and eyeliner. It was tasteful, but I knew she had done it just for the attractive Phillip Howell. And she probably knew I knew.

"I brought some donuts. Fried foods are good for arcane sickness, you know."

Howell pointed to the paper bag on the counter. "I brought her a couple as well, but more wouldn't hurt."

"Smart man," my mother said, giving me a look that clearly said she approved. "I've got some of my special healing cream, too. Made a fresh batch this morning after Phillip told me about the tough day you had last night."

I glared at Howell behind my mother's back as I opened the box and inspected the contents. These had sprinkles. "What exactly did Phillip tell you about yesterday?"

"Oh, something about an arrest at a bar and then a fight with someone last night." She sniffed at the air. "He didn't mention the demon getting into your house, though."

I choked on a donut. "How did you—"

"Ava, please. Once you've smelled a demon, you never forget it. And no amount of deodorizing spray is going to get the smell out soon." She sighed. "You're here, and you're not too badly beat up, so I can only assume it was a fairly weak one and you were able to banish it easily enough?"

I nodded, hoping Howell wouldn't contradict me. "It was only here for a moment or two. No harm, other than a few bruises and a broken front door."

"Someone you arrested sent it after you?" She pulled an

unlabeled white jar from her handbag and twisted the lid off.

I nodded, taking another bite to keep myself from talking too much.

"Well, they didn't do themselves any favors, sending a demon after you. I'm sure you'll figure out who sent it and arrest them." She held my chin while she dabbed a small amount of her amazing cream around my black eye. "Though I wish you hadn't gone into police work. I've always said it was too dangerous."

"Actually, I quit."

There was maybe a full second of silence before my mother let out a long sigh and quirked an eyebrow. "Good."

I have to admit, I was a little surprised. "You're not going to ask me why, or bother me about what I'm going to do for a job now?"

She shrugged. "No. Whatever it is, I bet it's safer than working for the APD." She passed the white tub to me. "You have no idea how many times I was up late watching the news when I knew you were on a big case, just to make sure nothing bad happened to you. The further away you stay from the police, the happier I'll be."

Howell shifted uncomfortably. Janet huffed and collapsed at his feet.

The noise drew my mother's attention, and she made a delighted squeal. "Well, who is this adorable little sweetheart?" She knelt to fawn over Janet and her large belly, and I took the chance to make my exit.

"I'll just go put some of this on a few other spots." I waved the tub for no one in particular, making my way back to my bedroom. "Behave yourself, Mother."

I took my time with the task, listening for my mother's voice. I felt guilty for not admitting that I fully intended to continue working closely with the police, just not as a detective. And not with the APD. I could only rationalize it by telling myself that any intention I had of becoming a consultant for the Norman Police Department may not pan out. There was no need to give her reason to worry when nothing may come of my half-baked plans.

Better not to mention it at all, I finally decided.

"She's gone, Maxwell. You can stop hiding now." Howell's voice came from the front hall, where he had evidently just finished walking my mother out to her car.

I re-entered the living room and kitchen area. "Sorry. I didn't really mean to leave you out here with her like that." I snagged another donut, wiping residual medicinal cream from my hand onto my pants before squeezing out jelly filling and licking my fingers. "She can be a strange one sometimes."

"She's a character, alright." Howell opened the back door for Janet again, and she wobbled her way outside. "She strongly suggested I ask either you or her out on a date."

I wrinkled my nose. "Either of us?"

Howell laughed. "She prioritized you." He shrugged. "I had to politely decline, of course. Janet is about all the female companionship I can handle at the moment."

Howell and I spent a few minutes measuring and picking out a replacement for my front door. When we exited through the garage to make our way to the hardware store, I was surprised to see an oversized van in my driveway. It dwarfed my little Blackbird, and looked to be one of those triple-row seaters with massive storage in the back.

"Is this yours?" I asked Howell as he opened the side door and helped Janet up into the seats.

"Nah, it's my sister's. I took chaperone duty for my niece's soccer practice this morning."

I pointed to a small black cleat sticking out from under one of the seats. "Someone left a shoe behind."

Howell sighed. "That would be Abby. She always leaves something. I'll give her mom a call later."

I settled into the passenger seat, and Janet immediately rested her head on my shoulder. I gave the sweet girl a nose rub. "So, you're helping your sister out with your niece?"

Howell buckled in and started the engine. "Yeah. She got a divorce last year, and it's been tough on both of them." He twisted in his seat, bracing his hand on the back of my headrest as he backed out of the driveway. I got a whiff of something spicy and slightly musky from Howell. Deodorant, likely. Janet's head, still resting on my shoulder, was an inch or so below Howell's arm. He gave her a pat as he twisted forward again. "So I asked for a transfer from my office in Chicago to down here, pulled a couple of strings with some fed guys I know, and landed something better and closer to Jessie and my sister." Howell shrugged. "Rented an apartment a quarter mile away from their house, packed Janet up, and hit the road."

"I bet your sister is happy to have her big brother here to help out," I said.

"Little brother," Howell corrected with a smile. "And she was pissed at first. Thought I was throwing my career away to help her out. But Jessie loves having her uncle Phillip around, and I'm happier with my career path here than I was back in Chicago."

We chatted amicably the rest of the drive to the hardware store. Howell chose the same one I had gone to yesterday afternoon, and this time I was able to navigate the store more confidently. With no need. Howell seemed to know the place like the back of his hand, and he even greeted a few staff members by name.

We were inside for less than ten minutes before walking

out with everything needed to replace the door. Janet greeted us at the van with an excited bark, and when Howell asked her to help unload, she took the plastic bag he offered her and set it between the front seats.

"You want some fried chicken?" Howell asked. "I think that place you like is close by." He smiled. "And fried foods are good for arcane sickness."

My mouth was already salivating. "I was hoping you would ask."

Howell, it turned out, was quite skilled at handiwork. I had a general idea of how to patch cracked drywall, but Howell showed me how to fill larger spots. He worked his magic on the door jamb while I alternated between sitting on the couch in a sweaty mess and eating various forms of fried carbohydrates while standing in the kitchen. We also replaced the trim, and before the afternoon had entirely given way to evening, I had a brand-new door. It was unpainted, but I liked the idea of giving it some color myself.

We sat on the couch, each holding a cold beer, with Janet lying on the floor between our feet. I propped my feet up on the coffee table. "How long have we known each other now, Howell?"

Howell made a show of looking at his watch. "About thirty-six hours."

I laughed.

* * *

The next morning, I woke up at a far more reasonable hour. I made a pot of coffee, ate a staling donut, and sat down to give Freya a call.

"This is *The Quill*, Freya speaking. How can I enchant your day?"

"Hi Freya, it's Ava."

"Ava!" Her tone instantly shifted from a light and bubbly customer service voice to the warm and rich voice I recognized from the other day. "How are you feeling? Are you taking care of yourself?"

"I am, thank you for asking." I set my donut aside and leaned back into the couch cushions. "And thank you for calling Howell, I'd like to add. He babied me all day yesterday. Even got my mother in on it."

"Good. You seem like the kind of person that doesn't know the meaning of 'self-care', so I thought you might need some extra help."

I rolled my eyes. She wasn't wrong. I couldn't remember the last time I'd had a relaxing day to myself. "Howell said you wanted me to call when I was feeling better. Something about a job you might have for me?"

"It depends." Her voice was coy. "Are you up for a hike?"

I was at *The Quill* a short time later. Freya gave me the gate code to the small employee parking area behind the small strip her shop stood in. There were a couple of neutral and nondescript sedans parked towards the end, and I guessed they belonged to the employees of the Asian restaurant that took up roughly half of the strip. The other end, which housed a storefront I vaguely remembered having a 'For Lease' sign in the window, was empty. And I spotted what could only be Freya's car parked right in the middle of the parking lot. It was a medium shade of orange, with a silver and blue decal that announced it was an all-electric vehicle. There was also a bumper sticker that read "I brake for butterflies" and a magnet for her own shop.

I paused to take a look at the magnet. The letters were too stylized to make out properly. I still couldn't tell if it was supposed to read *The Quill and Kettle* or *The Quill and Cauldron*. I made a mental note to ask Freya. I walked around the building from the empty storefront end and went inside.

Freya wasn't alone when I entered. She stood in front of the counter, leaning against it casually. She wore a cute sleeveless dress in a pale green that complimented her red hair nicely. It had a pleated skirt and small pink and red flowers embroidered along the hem. She'd paired it with small and soft-looking taupe booties.

Freya had wonderful legs, and I had to keep myself from staring at them as she turned to greet me.

"Ava! I'm glad you made it." She reached out for what I thought was going to be a side hug, but instead turned into her looping her arm through mine and half escorting me, half showing me off to the other store patrons. "How was riding down here on the bike with your arm?"

"Oh, it was fine," I answered. "The shoulder pain is gone, actually."

I didn't want to admit that I had jostled it painfully when I'd inadvertently ridden over a bump in the road a little too fast. The pain really was mostly gone, but every once in a while I got an unpleasant reminder that it had been popped out of its socket not too long ago.

"Ava, these are the Bryants, Robert and Leslie. They're the ones interested in hiring you."

I shook their hands. Mr. Bryant was an approachable sort of guy. He had a warm smile and a teasing glint in his eyes when he looked over at Mrs. Bryant. His wife was not all that different, and there was a mischievous quirk to her grin. They gave off the air of being a couple that had known each other for decades and would become more and more alike as they aged.

I liked them instantly.

"I understand you need some help with something you've lost?"

"Not something *we* lost, actually. Something a friend of ours lost," Robert said.

"Okay." I shrugged. "Shouldn't be too difficult. Tell me about this thing you lost."

"It's a pair of glasses," Leslie said with a smirk. "They were lost while hiking in the Wichitas."

I paused, looking at Freya. She gave me a wink and I sighed. "Alright, I'll bite. Why are you wanting to find these glasses? Were the frames made of gold?"

That got a laugh out of both Bryants.

"Actually, if you don't find them, that's fine. We're just curious what happened to them," Robert said.

"Though it would be hilarious if we could bring them back to Derrick after all these years," Leslie added.

"Okay, I think I might need the whole story." I leaned against the counter, giving Freya a sideways look. I wasn't entirely convinced someone wasn't trying to play a joke on me.

Robert instantly lit up as if he had been waiting for the chance to tell the tale. "Well, every year, we get together with a group of friends and all take a trip down to the Wichita Mountains. The hikes are great, the weather is normally cooperative, and it's a good opportunity for us to get back together and catch up."

"Usually," Leslie interjected with an arch of an eyebrow.

Robert tilted his head, accepting her comment, and continued. "One year we went down there, and our friend Derrick took a tumble during the hike. He was fine, nothing worse than a few scrapes. But he lost his glasses in the fall, and we spent an hour looking. Never found them. Derrick spent the rest of the hike half blind, being guided back down the mountain by the pair of us and another friend."

"Talk about a bonding experience," I said.

"It became a running joke." Leslie picked up the story

with only little less excitement than Robert had displayed. "We'd get to the spot where Derrick fell and tell everyone with us to keep an eye out for a pair of glasses."

"And they were never found?"

They both shook their heads.

"We never really expected to find them. It just became another memory of a hike from years ago," Robert said.

I exchanged another look with Freya. Her eyes had a strange look to them, but she said nothing. "How long ago are we talking?"

Robert and Leslie both gave the questions a few seconds of thought.

"Twenty years?" Robert said.

"Twenty-three, I think," Leslie amended.

"Fuck." I turned to Freya. "You're joking, right? I don't think that's possible."

"Oh, come on, Ava!" Freya gave my uninjured arm a gentle tug. "It's not like they want you to come back with the glasses fully intact or anything."

"You could come back completely empty-handed, honestly. We'd still pay you just for giving it a try," Leslie said.

I narrowed my eyes at the couple. "You'd be willing to pay me even if I don't find these glasses?"

Robert nodded. "Mileage, expenses, and two fifty just for taking the job. And an extra five hundred if you actually find them."

I whistled. *Two hundred and fifty dollars to take a hike in the Wichita Mountains?*

"Get it in writing, and you have a deal."

"Done." Freya produced a slip of paper from the top of the counter with a flourish. It was short and handwritten, with three signatures and a spot for a fourth.

I took the paper and read it over. It was all there.

Mileage rate at fifty cents to the mile, the option to take expenses or a forty dollar per diem, whichever was lower, and a bonus payout for collecting the glasses. "How did you know I was going to take this job?"

Freya shrugged. "You seem like the type to take on fun jobs."

I inspected the signatures. Robert had signed first, followed by his wife Leslie. And then Freya had signed as a witness in an ornate signature that matched the handwriting on the agreement. There was no last name listed.

I sighed, then penned my own signature with the ballpoint Freya held out for me. "Alright, no promises on bringing the glasses back. But to do this properly, I need a few things from you guys."

"Something connecting the owner to the glasses?" Leslie suggested.

I gave Freya yet another look. She shrugged innocently, but the corners of her mouth pulled gently up into a smile.

"Yeah. The case they were kept in, for example."

Robert nodded. "We asked Derrick about the case, but he tossed it long ago." He pulled out a plain black eyeglass case and handed it to me. "So I thought this might work instead? It's the pair he bought to replace the ones he lost in the mountains. He wore them for about fifteen years, then got corrective surgery."

"Hm." I opened the case. The glasses inside were plain metal frames. Boring, silver frames with thick lenses. "It might work." I looked to Freya. "What do you think?"

She shook her head. "I think this is your case to figure out. I helped out on the last one. I'm sitting this one out."

"Gee, thanks."

I turned back to the frames. With a quick blink, I did my little arcane scan. There was a good deal of residual energy on the glasses. Interestingly, the energy was focused on the lenses, not the frames, as if Derrick didn't really care about the way the frames looked, only that the glasses helped him to see. I blinked again, dismissing the spell that let me see the aura surrounding the glasses.

"I think these will work. Does Derrick need them back?"

Robert and Leslie both shook their heads.

"Freya, do you have a small jar? Preferably something with a twist cap? Two, actually."

While Freya disappeared into the back storage room, I popped the lenses out of the glasses and carefully marked an arrow from the center to an outer edge on each lens. "Thank you, Robert and Leslie. I'll start on this immediately. Let's meet back here in ..." I paused, clicking my tongue as I thought. "Four days. I'll have Freya call you to set up a time."

We parted soon after. Freya had just the kind of jars I was hoping she would have, and I dropped a lens into each one. She would only give them to me if I promised to celebrate taking my first freelance job by going out to dinner with her the following weekend. As excited as I was by the prospect of having a date with her, I couldn't help but hesitate before agreeing.

As soon as I got home, I started packing. I also gave Frankie a call.

He answered with his usual greeting: "Yeah, bitch?"

"Hey, I know this is short notice, but would you like to go camping with me?"

"Hmm. When are you leaving?"

"In an hour?" I stared at the mess of camping supplies around me. I was surprised to realize I owned most everything I needed already. Likely because much of it doubled as severe weather gear. The camping lanterns, for example, I'd definitely bought after an unpleasant evening spent in my storm shelter in the dark. "I need to go pick up a tent, but I should be finished packing soon."

"I have a tent, if you don't mind sharing."

"So you'll come?" I let out a relieved sigh. I had expected Frankie to decline, but I didn't really feel comfortable wandering unfamiliar hiking trails on my own.

"Sure. You sound a little stressed, and you're not the type to make last-minute camping plans."

"I just took a job down in the Wichita Mountains. I was going to camp tonight and start the job in the morning."

"Alright. You finish packing, I'll call the camp and make a site reservation."

"You're my hero, Frankie."

"Just get me home before the weekend is over, and we'll be just fine. I could use some time out of the house. I'm so sick of grading these lousy-ass lab reports."

We left a little more than an hour later. Frankie and I stopped for lunch before even leaving Norman city limits, and I shared the events of the last two days with him over a burger and fries.

"Two fifty to take a hike in the mountains? Damn," Frankie said as he dipped a few short fries into a sauce cup.

"That's what I said." I wiped a dribbling mess of blended ketchup and mayonnaise from my palm. "And an extra five hundred if I find the glasses."

"Damn," Frankie repeated.

"I'll pass the mileage money on to you, since you're driving, and if we find the glasses, I'll split the five hundred."

"Deal." Frankie leaned back in his chair. "You know how you're going to try to find them?"

I nodded. "I have the lenses from the pair this Derrick guy bought to replace the lost glasses. I was going to make a kind of compass from them."

"Get them to lead us to the lost ones?"

"If it works." I shrugged. "It's been so long, and there isn't really a direct relationship between the two pairs."

"Only one way to find out."

The Wichita Mountains were really only about a ninety-minute drive from Norman. Even with Frankie driving painfully slow at the exact speed limit, not even a single mile per hour over, we got to our campsite with hours before sunset.

I was determined to start searching for the glasses immediately, but Frankie was insistent that we take the evening to hike some smaller trails and relax before settling in for the night.

"It'll give us time to plan the hike for tomorrow," he said.

And, though I didn't want to admit it, I wasn't too sure I was completely back to normal after my blessedly short bout of arcane sickness.

Frankie picked a short trail from a map he pulled up on his cell phone. It was an easy hike, with very little steep climbing. I was mildly surprised to see cacti along the trail paths. There was a great deal of wildlife as well, and I took a photo of a cluster of interesting flowers I didn't recognize to identify later.

"We should have brought some fishing gear. We could have stopped to get a day license and made an afternoon of it."

I laughed, imagining Frankie, usually a fastidious clean freak, hauling fishing gear. "I didn't know you fished."

"I don't usually. Dorian hates it. Too smelly, too hot, too many worms to touch." He gave me a hand over a gap in the path where an earthquake or some other event had created a crack several inches deep and several more wide. "But I've always liked it. It's peaceful."

"But you guys go camping together all the time. He's never been fishing with you?"

"Girl, most of our camping is for outdoor festivals." Frankie laughed at me. "I wouldn't be surprised if my sleeping bag still had glitter in it from the last one."

"Dorian doesn't like camping, either?"

Frankie shook his head. "Too dirty, too many bugs, and no electricity." He paused, pointing out a hawk flying close by. "He loves renting cabins and going off grid for a week or so at a time, though. We do that every summer, and I get some fishing in then. It's perfect."

I knew about the off-grid time at the cabin. Frankie and Dorian had a standing rental every year for the same one. It sounded nice, and they always came back like they had just spent a week on honeymoon. I was honestly a little jealous. I would do the same, but I would get horribly bored on my own and cut the week short.

Maybe Freya would enjoy a vacation like that ...

Our hike finished with little trouble. I was sweating and thirsty by the time we reached the end of the trail, but I had a strange sense of accomplishment and a good deal of energy. The energy quickly faded into groans of pain from muscle aches as Frankie and I made dinner. Frankie had brought a small camping grill, and he warmed hotdogs and buns over a tiny propane flame. The condiments came from restaurant packets. It was the best damned hotdog I'd ever eaten.

I set an alarm, keeping my phone plugged into a battery backup in case it wanted to die overnight. Frankie's sleeping bag did indeed have a small amount of glitter tucked into the inner corners, so he opted to sleep on top of it and covered himself with a wool blanket he'd brought.

The night sounds were pleasant, and either because of the hike or my lingering arcane fatigue, I fell asleep quickly.

* * *

Our hike the next day was not as easy or pleasant as the first one had been. I had studied the map carefully, but the spot the Bryants had pointed out was not on any conventional trail. It was also on the far side of the mountain Frankie and I were climbing, so we would already be exhausted by the time we even reached the spot where I would need to start searching.

So we went off road a little. And regretted it almost immediately. Surprisingly sturdy thorn bushes tore at my clothing and hair, and the climb was deceptively steeper than it looked. When we reached the top of the mountain, sweaty and covered in small cuts, we stopped for a break.

"How long have we been out here?" I asked.

Frankie glanced at his watch. He didn't normally wear one, but he had brought some fancy one with a built-in compass just for today. I was grateful for the foresight.

"Two hours."

"Not bad." I chugged some water. My first bottle was nearly empty, but I had two more in the backpack I carried.

"It's a six-hour trail."

"Shit."

We ate a couple of granola bars as we bird-watched for a few moments and let the light breeze congeal the sweat on our bodies before continuing on.

The cacti grew more thickly on the far side of the mountain than they had on the way up. The wildlife was larger than what we had seen the day before, too. I spotted a pair of deer, and Frankie and I watched them run and bounce away from sight when they noticed our presence.

I paused on the trail, taking a deep breath of the pine-scented air. "I think I might like to come back and do this climb again sometime," I told Frankie. "Maybe take the proper trail up instead of struggling through the brush."

Frankie gave me a dirty and exhausted look. "Tell me how you feel after your second wind fades."

My second wind faded moments before we reached our next resting point. I dropped my backpack onto the ground and leaned against a large outcrop of rock. "Fuck, I'm never hiking again." Sweat was accumulating in the brim of my baseball cap, and I pulled it off to wipe at my forehead.

"There's the Ava I know." Frankie tossed me a granola bar. "Where are we starting our search? Is it close?"

I smacked the outcrop I leaned against. "Our story apparently starts right here."

"Oh?"

"The more detailed story I got from the Bryants is that this used to be the entrance to a small cave. It's collapsed due to earthquakes, but at one point you could rappel down into it and then climb back out through a hole on the other side."

Frankie squinted at me as he tore a small piece of granola from his bar and ate it. "Sounds weird, but alright."

"It was shortly after they had climbed back out of the cave that Derrick fell and lost his glasses." I pointed down a steep and gravelly slope. "We go down there and around to the right a bit, and we'll end up right in front of what used to be the cave exit. I can get everything ready to start the search now, though." I shrugged. "No telling where the glasses may have been carried off to after all these years."

"Alright." Frankie brushed a few crumbs from his hands and pocketed the granola wrapper. "I'm game. Let's get started."

I retrieved both jars containing the lenses from my backpack. Frankie took one in each hand and held them steady for me as I uncapped them and filled the jars about three quarters full of water. With the caps twisted back into place, I flipped a jar over. The bottom was clear plastic, and the water let the lens float. A quick swirl of the jar made sure the lens, with the arrow drawn on its surface, could spin freely.

It took a little more effort on my part than it should have, but I was able to spark the spell needed to tie the lens in my hand to its lost predecessor. I passed the jar to Frankie and repeated the spell on the second lens.

Frankie was already turning in a slow circle, trying to get a lock on the location for the missing glasses. "I think we might have a problem."

I started turning in my own slow circle. "What's that?" The arrow on the lens pointed down the gravel path, then spun slightly to point off close to the way we had come.

"I'm getting two signals."

I sighed.

Frankie was facing a different direction than I was, glancing from his jar to the sealed entrance to the old rappelling cave. "Make that three signals. Maybe more." He looked up at me. "How do you want to go about this?"

I considered for a moment, taking another slow turn to determine how many signals I could pick up. It was definitely three. "We could split up?"

Frankie made a face. "And I get a guilty conscience when you slip and bust your head open because I'm not there to catch you? Bitch, please."

I ignored the mild irritation at being the one in need of saving in his scenario, but the point still stood. "Alright, then we just start with the one back the way we came and work our way down the mountain."

It wasn't a large backtrack, fortunately. But it was hard to pinpoint the precise spot that the lenses in our jars seemed to be responding to. There was a small gap between two large boulders, and after a quick game of Rock-Paper-Scissors, Frankie was the one unlucky enough to have to stick his hand inside. A precursory check with the flashlight on my phone showed no immediate danger, but I still cursed when Frankie let out a pained inhale of breath.

When he retracted his arm, a tiny piece of glass was stabbed into the meat of his hand.

"Man, now I gotta go get a tetanus booster." He dropped the glass shard into my hand. "Looks like part of a lens."

The glass was slightly curved, and there was a beveled edge. "One down, I guess. Not exactly the whole lens, but we'll make do."

Frankie squirted water onto his cut hand. "You're welcome to stick your hand in there and see what you can pull out."

"I've got a first-aid kit, hang on." I dropped my backpack and retrieved the kit. After depositing the piece of glass inside the metal case, I fished out an alcohol wipe, a tub of antibiotic ointment, and a large bandage with a cartoon mouse on the outside.

"You can't just do some magic voodoo to make the cut heal?" Frankie eyed the bandage. "Or at least give me an adult bandage?"

"Nope." I opened the alcohol wipe and passed it to him. "You get what you get, sorry."

The second signal was coming from a little further along the trail, down the gravel slope that would eventually lead us around to where the glasses were originally lost.

I lost my balance as we descended, slipping on the loose gravel. One foot slid into a thin rut and twisted slightly. I went down hard, and several sharp pains in my left ass cheek alerted me to the fact that I had inadvertently fallen onto a partially hidden cactus.

"Fuck." I held out a hand for Frankie. "I just turned my butt into a pincushion. Help me up."

Frankie was trying desperately to keep a straight face as he pulled me to my feet, but lost his composure as I carefully pulled needles from the seat of my pants. "I'd offer to help, but I just really don't want to."

"Then start tracking the next piece while I try to get myself sorted here, jackass." I turned to the cactus. It was a little bent, and there was a noticeable patch bare of needles. I glared at the offending plant and continued pulling needles from my rear. They were longer than I had expected, some as long as three inches, and horribly sharp. Those came out easily enough. But I could tell there were several I wasn't going to be able to remove just yet. "Tonight's shower will be an interesting one."

"Down here, Miss Prickly Pear. I think I know where the next piece is."

I followed the sound of Frankie's voice until I spotted him again. He stood at the base of a tall tree of some variety that I wasn't familiar with. Not an evergreen—that was as much as I could tell. The branches were bare, though I spotted a large clump of twigs and leaves in the branches.

Frankie was staring up at the tree, and I squinted up at it as well. "What is it?"

"That's a hawk nest."

"Yeah?"

Frankie showed me the jar he held. The arrow pointed steadily at the tree. "I tried to get a lock, but it just seems to point right at the tree."

I took a quick walk around the tree. He was right. With each step, the arrow on the lens pointed at the tree. "So it's in that nest?"

Frankie nodded. "Probably a piece of the frame."

I sighed. "There's no point in even thinking about retrieving it."

There goes the five hundred bucks for finding the whole pair.

I doubted the Bryants would have paid the bonus anyway, seeing as we had only collected a piece of one lens so far.

"Alright. Last spot, I guess."

We took the trail down and around the collapsed cave entrance we had paused at earlier. The path flattened out for about a hundred feet, then abruptly fell away into a series of large boulders that were settled on a steep decline. There was a small second path that branched off to the left, but of course the arrow on our arcane compasses pointed stubbornly down the more hazardous trail.

Frankie and I exchanged a look. He rolled his eyes. "I'll go first."

"My hero."

After hopping the first few boulders, the rest were easy. They were much larger on top than they first appeared, and my ankle was fine despite my fall earlier. The arrow swiveled around suddenly as we hopped the last boulder and back onto solid ground.

Frankie shook his head. "I stuck my hand into the last creepy hole. You get this one."

"But I fell on a cactus," I whined.

"Don't care."

"Oh fine." I turned the flashlight on my cell phone on once more and knelt down to inspect the area around the final boulder. There was a small gap just under the rock, but the hole was too small and too poorly angled for me to get a look under it. After a brief hesitation, I stuck a few fingers under.

There was something warm and furry in there, and I shrieked and pulled away. A rodent, something roughly the size of a rat, scurried out from under the boulder and ran off.

Frankie laughed as I tried to get my heart rate under control.

"What the heck was that thing?" I asked, staring in the direction the little creature had run off in.

"Nothing that will kill you. I feel bad for him, honestly."

I had too much adrenaline coursing through me to feel bad for the little animal. I took a deep breath and stuck my fingers inside the hole again. It was a tight fit. The gap between rock and earth wasn't large enough for me to reach my entire hand in, but I could feel *something* just at my fingertips.

"Can you find me a little stick?" I asked Frankie, looking over my shoulder at him.

He already had one held out for me, and I used it to do a kind of sweep under the rock.

A round piece of glass slid out from under the stone. It was dirty and dusty, and there were a couple of small chips, but it was relatively intact.

"Yes!" I scooped the lens up and inspected it.

"Does this mean we can go back to the campsite now?" Frankie asked.

I took my backpack off and pulled out the first-aid kit. "Looks like it. How long have we been up here?"

"Five hours or so."

"And how much longer do you think it'll take to get back to the camp?" I tucked the lens in with the shard of its companion and sealed the kit once more.

Frankie pulled out his phone and hit a few quick buttons. "Two hours?"

"Alright." I put my backpack on and adjusted the straps. "Let's book it, boyo."

* * *

We finished the trail in a little less than two hours, and we were home again after another two and a half. Frankie dropped me off at home and immediately made for the apartment he and Dorian shared after little more than a short farewell. I couldn't blame him. It had been a long day, and he looked exhausted. I made a mental note to thank him properly again the next day.

I called Freya before doing anything else.

She answered on the second ring. "Ava?"

"Yeah, it's me."

"How was your hiking trip?" It could have been a polite conversation starter, but Freya sounded genuinely curious and interested.

"It was fruitful, surprisingly. But I'm pretty beat." I opened the first-aid kit and pulled out the nearly intact lens Frankie and I had found. "Can you call the Bryants and schedule a time to meet at your shop? My schedule is wide open. You can text me on this number with the details. Whatever works for them is fine with me."

"Great! And how does some Italian sound for dinner next Saturday night? Seven p.m., let's say?"

I smiled. "It sounds good."

I showered after we hung up. I was covered in dirt and sweat and I still had several small cactus needles stuck to my rear, which I was for some reason embarrassed about. It was a long, hot shower, and I fell into bed and slept deeply afterwards.

* * *

"And that's how it was found," I said to the Bryants.

Leslie passed the lens to Robert, who stared at it in wide-eyed surprise.

He laughed, the big belly-laugh sort that was shorter than it should have been. "I can't believe you found even this much of it."

"Oh, there is a second piece." I pulled out a small wad of tissue paper. "This one has some sharp edges, though. Be careful."

"There's more?" Leslie asked. She was smiling. "This is great!"

"It's just a piece from the other lens. We were able to track down another part of it, but it seemed to have been incorporated into a hawk's nest, so we didn't bother trying to retrieve it."

"No kidding." Robert held the lens up to his eye and peered through it. "I wonder if the rest was lost in a rainstorm or during an earthquake. I honestly thought you would return empty-handed." He gave me a wink. "No offense. But it's been over twenty years."

"I thought I would return empty-handed too, actually."

"Alright," Freya piped up from behind the counter. She held a calculator in one hand and a pen in the other. "I've totaled up Ava's expenses and calculated her mileage reimbursement." She wrote a number on the bottom of my itemized report and showed it to Leslie.

The only thing I had expensed was the cheeseburger I ate on the way out to the mountains. I didn't even include the drink and fries. It felt weird.

"Do you do PayFriends?" Leslie asked, pulling out her phone.

I did the same. "Sure." I gave her my email address for the lookup.

Leslie hit several buttons, showed the screen to Robert,

who nodded approval, and then made one final tap on her screen.

A notification immediately popped up on my phone. The banner read *You've received a payment of $800 from RobnLes. Accept your money now!*

I blinked. "I can't take that much."

"Sure you can," Robert said. "You earned the bonus."

I scoffed. "No, I didn't. I didn't find the glasses in their entirety."

"The job contract didn't say you had to find the glasses in their entirety," Leslie said. "It just said to find them. You've found one entire lens, a significant chunk from the other lens, and you said you tracked another part of the glasses to a hawk's nest. I think that more than qualifies."

"You're kidding."

"Take the money, Ava," Robert said. "Seriously. You did an amazing job. And we have your email if we ever need your help with this sort of thing again."

I had this weird, warm sensation in my chest. It took a second for me to realize I was about to start weeping. A stranger had just given me a sincere compliment, and I was about to bawl about it.

I accepted the payment and cleared my throat. "Well, thank you for your business. I'd love to work with you again, if you need me. Oh, and I almost forgot about these guys." I pulled the two jars containing the newer lenses out of my jacket pocket and set them on Freya's counter. The insides were still damp, but they were no worse for wear. "A bit of nail polish remover will get the sharpie right off, and then you can probably just pop them back into the frames and return them to Derrick."

I gave the Bryants an awkward wave. "I hope you don't mind, but I need to go see my mother about a recipe for pain cream."

I exited the shop before I could make a further fool of myself and quickly walked around the building and to my Blackbird. I sent Frankie three hundred bucks via PayFriends—half the bonus plus gas mileage. He texted me a string of emojis right away. There was a tree and some birds and a smiley face with hearts for eyes. And then a money bag. And some other characters I didn't care to try to decipher.

Maybe this freelancing thing would work out alright after all.

ABOUT THE AUTHOR

Jacklyn Hennion is an avid lover of sweets and wine. She enjoys Netflix and video games, and often spends the evenings winding down with a bit of crochet work. She and her husband currently live in Oklahoma. *Settling Dust* is Jacklyn's fourth published novel, and her first urban fantasy.

Also by Jacklyn Hennion

The Book of Death

The Book of Water

The Book of Fire

www.ingramcontent.com/pod-product-compliance
Lightning Source LLC
Chambersburg PA
CBHW030631190726
48286CB00008B/2474